MW01595033

MISSION OF LOVE

Sabrina Johnson Fye

Copyright © 2022 Sabrina Johnson Fye
All rights reserved
The characters and events portrayed in this book are fictitious. Any similarity to real persons, living or dead, is coincidental and not intended by the author.
No part of this book may be reproduced, or stored in a retrieval system, or transmitted in any form or by any means, electronic, mechanical, photocopying, recording, or otherwise, without express written permission of the publisher.

ISBN-13: XXXXXXX
Printed in the United States of America

DEDICATION

This book is dedicated to my four daughters. Mother's Day morning 2018, my bedroom was bombrushed and I was showered with gifts. One being a laptop along with the message" We're grown now, it's time to write". Following their inspiration, I began to write. Therefore, I am dedicating the first book of the series to them. Thank you ladies, for believing in me. I hope that I made you proud.

Mama

CHAPTER ONE

"Nate, please," begged Chief Louis.

"Naw … naw chief, I'm done! My retirement is within two months. I have put in my time.

Now you're asking for another mission? Never! I should have suspected that it was something work-related when you asked me to meet you here, at the office. I think that I've given the SEALS more than enough of my life; I'd like to enjoy the rest of it," said Nate.

"But this isn't just another mission, Nate! My problem is, I can't just send anybody! This mission requires skills, intelligence and heart. Do I have other agents available to go?

Yes. Do I want them to? No!

"I need someone swift, sharp and quick on his feet...I choose you. I know all about the retirement thing and that's why I've come, prepared to sweeten the offer. This is it: you do this for me. If you take the mission, as soon as it is accomplished, I will have you processed and out within two weeks. Full retirement," explained Lou.

"Seriously?" questioned Nate.

"Seriously, no red tape," averred Lou.

They shook on it and discussed a few details. Two weeks later, Nate found himself in a remote location, 1,500 feet in the air, about to solo dive into his next mission. Like many other times before, the dive was a success, landing him right in the middle of the expected area outside of the compound. Lou had only given him a brief overlook into the mission. That's what made him skeptical—he hated going into situations blindly.

Moving toward the compound, he found a tree with lots of branches and a canopy top. He decided to make it his contact zone. Quickly, he scrambled to the top of the tree and secured his backpack to his body by the straps. Then, he secured his duffle bag, which contained other beneficial items, to a neighboring branch. He changed his shirt and scrambled back down, with a map between his teeth.

The directions that Lou had given him were on point! It led him directly into the back of the compound. Nate's previous two weeks of running and cross training seemed to be paying off! He was amazed at how quickly he'd arrived. He stopped a few feet away from the compound door. Taking a moment to gather himself, he took a deep breath and said a quick prayer. "Oh Gracious Father, keep me and protect me. Use me to do whatever it is that you brought me here for, in Jesus' name... Amen.

"Oh, and Lord ... please don't let me have to kill anybody, so tired of that ... Amen."

He approached the door and banged on it loudly!

"Who are you?" came a voice from the other side.

"Yeah, the name is Blue," said Nate.

He tapped "man three" in Morse code. Immediately, the door swung open and Nate entered the musty, dark hallway. It took a moment for his eyes to adjust.

"Ha—man, are we glad to see you," the man who opened the door said. "I'm 'Old J', Oscar Johnson, and this here is Moose. We call him that because he's Canadian."

"Really?" asked Nate.

"Pay this old man no mind." They all laughed.

"Well, they call me Blue, short for Code Blue. Yep, so they say ... these hands are a lethal weapon," chuckled Nate, admiring his hands.

"They who?" asked Moose.

"The judicial system ... yeah, these puppies have gotten me locked up a couple of times." Nate kissed his fists.

"Wow, man, remind me to stay on your good side."

Just by looking at him, Moose knew that Nate was a 6'3", 280 lb. wrecking ball that he did not want to tussle with! Nate said it as a joke, but everything he said was true. Without warning, he quickly clasped his big hands together, startling Moose and Old J!

"So what is it that you need me to do?" asked Nate.

"Well, first let me show you around. This old building is like a maze. I advise that you keep your gun and your flashlight handy at all times," suggested Old J.

"What is this place?" asked Nate.

"Oh, they say it belongs to the cartel, that it was one of their big smuggling warehouses back in the day. One of their underground hideaways."

"I see …"

"OK, now our quarters are on the second floor. The job is on the third floor," explained Old J.

"Well, being that this place was built into the mountain, the third floor would be ground level, right?"

"Right on, bro! I can see that we're gonna get along just fine; you're smart."

"Yep, well this is it! This is where you will be staying." He opened the massive iron door to the quarters. "It won't be so bad sharing, because only one of us will be here at a time. One of us will be on duty and the third person will be on ground patrol. Except for on Wednesdays, but I will let the boss man tell you about that! Meanwhile, let's go up to the third floor and see where you will be working." As the elevator door opened, all Nate could hear was the ungodly wailing of a woman!

"What is that?" he asked.

"Oh, my friend, that there is your job! See, we're here to guard her, so that she doesn't escape."

"Is she bound?" asked Nate.

"Yeah, she's confined to the bed. We must rotate the handcuffs from her hands to her feet. It allows her behind to breathe. It's a nice one, too."

Nate pretended that he didn't even hear that comment. It also made him wonder if they had been raping her. As Nate set up his workstation, he continued to ask questions.

"So who is the unlucky lady?"

"Oh, she's the 27-year-old daughter of a major big wheel. He owes the cartel a lot of money, something about a deal that went wrong. Anyway, from what I understand, the guy has already lost a finger and toe."

"Really," laughed Nate.

"Yep, from what I hear the big guy went up there to pay him a little visit. Apparently,

she came down to take a swim. Being the daddy's girl that she is, she came over to give him a kiss before heading out. Her dad saw the big guy getting an eyeful, so he offered her. She thinks that she's been kidnapped. Poor thing, has no idea that she was sold."

"What, sold?" questioned Nate.

"You heard me! Yes sir, the old man told the big guy that he could have her if he dropped all debts...wiped the slate clean! His only request was that it looked like a kidnapping. Guess he didn't want to face the Mrs." Old J explained.

"Idiot! That poor girl..." said Nate.

"The wailing is probably because she was taken during the night. They snatched her right out of her bed. Now it's our job to keep her, until they decide what they want to do with her."

"I take it she must be beautiful?"

"Yeah ... well, sort of," said Old J, trying to hold back his laugh.

"Well, my new friend, it's yours for the night. I'm out of here! Holla at you in the morning," said Old J chuckling as he opened the massive door that led to the elevators.

Something about that chuckle rubbed Nate the wrong way.

Man oh man, Lou, what have you gotten me into, said Nate to himself.

He was beginning to kick himself in the butt for taking this mission. Something was telling him this one was not going to be easy!

The woman wailed all night long. It was the sound of someone hurting, in pain, truly mourning. Nate had to talk himself through the night; by morning, his nerves were shot!

OK, Nate, man, up. She's not your sister, don't get soft. When you get soft, it's time to get out, he kept telling himself. Six a.m. sharp, the iron doors flew open.

"Thank God!" thought Nate, jumping to his feet.

"So, bro, how was your first night, are you ready for some sleep?" Moose greeted him sarcastically, grinning.

"Well, let's just say that she didn't sleep. She cried all night long! I mean, this woman could be an opera singer!"

Moose was laughing; but Nate failed to see the

humor. He quickly packed his things and decided to get out while he still had a chance.

"She's all yours now, man," said Nate as he hurried to the elevator, rubbing the curly black hair on his head.

"Get some sleep! It will be your turn again before you know it."

"Hasta la vista!" called Nate, as the elevator doors opened.

"This is going to be some well-deserved rest, he thought to himself as the elevator took him down to the second floor. Old J was leaving the quarters just as he stepped off the elevator.

"Going somewhere?" Nate asked.

"Yeah, think I will go hang out at the little pub shack down the way before I start patrol. It'll give me a chance to chat with the fellows and get me a shot or two before work. Man, do you need one?" Old J asked.

"Man, you said a mouthful! Good thing I'm not a drinking man," laughed Nate. "Does she cry all the time?"

"Yes, and when she's quiet, it scares me," Old J replied.

"How long is she going to be here?"

"Until they decide what they want to do with her. All I can say is, situations like this usually don't end well. On that note, guess I will go ahead and hit the sack. I need some shut eye, peace and quiet," said Nate, and they parted.

Nate slept like a rock. It was still several hours

before his shift began, but he couldn't stop thinking about her. He kept thinking about what Old J said earlier, too. He really needed to take a run to clear his head, but the South America heat made running a challenge. He lived for marathons, endurance running and cross training; his body confirmed it. He had the legs of a panther, strong and muscular. Something about running relaxed him. Nate was grateful for the night shift and intended to sneak out for a long run, as soon as he was familiar with the territory. For a while, he just laid in bed and meditated; trying to mentally prepare himself for another shift.

That night, Nate arrived about 20 minutes before shift change, to give himself a chance to chat with the guys and gather more information. When the elevator door opened, to his surprise, Nate found Moose coming out of the hostage's room, zipping up his pants. Nate's presence had startled him.

"Ha, Blue, you're here early; whatcha up to?" he asked.

"Nothing; just came down to chat with you guys for a minute," said Nate, closely watching Moose's fidgety and nervous demeanor.

"Are you going in," he said, gesturing toward the girl's door.

To hear him even say such rattled Nate to the core! He could literally feel his insides jumping! He had to suppress the urge to go over there and snap his neck!

"Naw man, I'm going to have to pass … I'm a respectful man, if you know what I mean," Nate declined.

"Yeah, oh yeah ... I can accept that," Moose replied. "Send the ole boy up when he comes out I'm out!"

"'K," said Nate. It was the only thing that he could get to escape his throat.

Whew, let me sit down! Lord, help me, please! I can see now, this is not gonna be good, thought Nate.

He sat down at the desk and put head in his hands, trying to wait for Old J to come out of the room. Nate was a bruiser, a true soldier, a warrior; but when it came to morals and matters of the heart, he was a big softie. His patience was wearing thin!

If he isn't out here in two minutes, I'm going in and it won't be to party, he said to himself!

As he sat there praying, he began to hear faint whimpers.

She's crying! OK, enough, he thought, slamming his hands down on the desk.

Just as he approached the door, it swung open. Old J came out, with a stupid look on his face. If only he knew how close he'd come to not having one!

"Ha there, big fellow, you going in?"

"No, thank you!" Nate growled, clenching his fists behind his back.

"Ha, well, it's up to you ... she's in there. We never know when they're going to decide what they wanna to do with her. Well, goodnight!"

"Sick Bastards," mumbled Nate under his breath, while repenting for cursing at the same time! How dare they act like she was a piece of property! She was a human being!

"Dear God, I need you! It's taking everything I got not to hurt these people, he cried out to the Lord.

Feeling sick to his stomach, he decided to sit down for a moment. That's when he heard it. Total silence! There was no crying, no moaning, no whimpering ... nothing. The silence made him nervous. He began to wonder if she was still alive.

Millions of thoughts began to rush through his mind. Nate knew that he needed to give her a visit and he needed to be prepared. He could only imagine what condition she was in. Nate walked over to the window and peered out. The sun was about to set.

"I don't want to leave her, but I don't have a choice," he said to himself.

Abandoning the girl, he decided to take a run to clear his head and get some supplies. Nate ran as hard and fast as he could. He made it to his tree and scrambled to the top like a spider monkey. He quickly unstrapped his bag and found his flashlight. It was the perfect time to be wearing cargo shorts! Stuffing two Capri Suns, a Z-pack (antibiotics), a bottle of water and crackers into his large pockets, he hurried down and headed back. Nate ran like lightning with jungle limbs smacking him as he whizzed by.

He slipped back into the compound undetected. Relieved that no one missed him, Nate said a prayer as he stood outside her door.

Then, following protocol, he pulled the black ski

mask over his face, unlocked the door and entered the room.

The odor met him at the door and astounded him. It was a poorly lit room. It was dirty, gloomy and rat feces were everywhere! A skilled soldier, it was natural for him to observe his surroundings. Nate swept the large room with his eyes until he found her.

The sight of her made him want to scream. There she was, a petite, small-framed woman. She was so frail that he could count each vertebra in her back. There she lay on a filthy bed with no sheets. Shackled by long chains like an animal, she laid in the fetal position sound asleep. The poor thing had burn marks all over her body. Her face, legs, back, buttocks, vagina, even the soles of her feet!

These idiots were actually using her as a human ashtray. They had been putting their cigarettes out on her! The numerous burns were disfiguring.. Wait. but neither Moose or Old J were smokers?. Which means someone else has been slipping in and out of her room, he thought

She was so exhausted she didn't even hear Nate enter the room. He stood there at the foot of her bed in silence. Slowly, she opened her eyes. Noticing yet another man standing there, she immediately leapt to her feet in the bed.

Her face looked like a pincushion. She could barely stand, as she was so weak.

Bracing herself against the wall, she faintly whispered, "No—no!"

Without saying a word, Nate threw up both of his hands in surrender. He slowly reached into his pocket and began to pull out the supplies. Out of fear, she continued to say no.

Nate shook his head while holding one finger to his lips. Pointing to his pocket with his free hand, he pulled out two small bananas he'd found on Moose's desk. She had to be famished! He hadn't seen anyone feed her since he'd arrived.

Nate threw the bananas on the bed in front of her. She grabbed, peeled and ate them at a pace that showed her desperation. She gobbled them down, while still keeping an eye on Nate, not completely trusting him.

Once she'd finished, again Nate slowly moved, pointing to the other pocket. This time, he could see the anticipation in her eyes. She was hoping that it was something else that she could eat.

He pulled out the crackers and Capri Sun, throwing them onto the bed. She grabbed them as soon as they hit the mattress. Last, Nate pulled out the Z-pack antibiotics and bottle of water. He didn't bother to open them, because he was still trying to gain her trust.

Just like everything else, he threw them on the bed before her. Then, he gestured to her to take them. She snatched the meds off the bed, looked at them both and then back at Nate. He again gestured for her to hurry up and take them. She caught on quickly. Reluctantly, she decided to take them; surely, she feared being drugged.

With shaky, trembling, filthy little hands, she struggled to open the medicine.

Nate so badly wanted to help her; but he dared not move.

So thirsty, she took the meds and finished off the water in a few big swallows. The poor thing was parched.

Time was of the essence. Nate knew he'd stayed too long and needed to get out of there. The last thing either one of them needed was for him to get caught.

So tired, yet grateful, all she could do was sit back on her heels, bowing to Nate with praying hands.

No! He didn't want praise! Not thinking, he reached towards her to help her up off her knees. Instead, the sudden motion scared her. She screamed as she scooted backwards, in retreat!

"Sh, shh," said Nate, shaking his head as he backed away

Now it was definitely time to get out of there! Nate quickly grabbed the banana peels and all the other trash off the bed, stuffing it back into his pockets. I can't leave any evidence, he thought. He checked under and around the bed, making sure that he had cleaned up everything, and prepared to exit.

Just as he was walking away, he stopped for a moment, turned and gestured for her to look into his eyes. She sat there motionless, as she stared into his big green eyes. They were kind eyes, she could tell he wasn't like the others ... this one was different. It was as if a huge sense of relief flooded them both and she relaxed. Without haste, Nate strode across the room, closed the door and locked it behind him. Then he sat down on the floor.

Whoever said that a man ain't supposed to cry lied. Tears flooded his eyes and despair filled his soul. He hadn't cried since he was fourteen and his father died. All that he could think about was her mother. He couldn't imagine the agony she must be going through as well. For a moment, it all became a little overwhelming, even for the big, buff soldier.

He had to reach into the corners of his mind to pull himself back together. Leaning against the door, he closed his eyes, trying to gather his thoughts. When he opened them, he was ready! He knew exactly what he was sent there to do.

"OK, game on...this means war! I need a plan," he said to himself.

CHAPTER TWO

The next few days were rough. Nate knew that he needed a plan and he needed one fast! He'd seen male prisoners tortured before, but never the females; nothing ever to this magnitude. Now, the mission was clear: he had to get her out.

Once again, he had to pull himself together and think of his next move. Implementing a plan had never been so hard to accomplish. All he could think about was her. He couldn't stop wondering if she was hurting; he knew that she had to be hungry and he could only pray that they weren't raping her again. Nate went to work that night with the intention of going to see her.

Unfortunately, he wasn't alone that night. One of the night patrol guys had an extreme case of laziness. He hid out in the office area and slept all night. It was another night of nothing but sheer silence. The thought of just sneaking in and out lingered in the back of Nate's mind all night. However, he remembered what his grandma always said...every closed eye ain't sleep. So instead, he chose to settle in his seat and do the only thing that he could do for her—pray. Between prayers and pleas with God, he listened. Come on, lady, scream, cry, moan … say something so that I know that you're alive, thought Nate.

Unfortunately, nothing, not a peep out of her all night. Instead, he was tortured by listening to this guy's snoring.

It was now Tuesday morning. Instead of going to bed when he got off, Nate planned to go to his tree and handle some business.

As he left the building, there stood three guys outside the compound door having an early smoke. In passing, Nate overheard them talking… He stopped, bent over and pretended to tighten the string in his boot.

"Yeah, man, Moose told us in a minute we won't have to worry about all that crying anymore."

"Really? Man, I hope so…I get tired of listening to it!"

"Yeah, well she will be gone soon."

"What do you mean, gone?"

"They made the decision to kill her! They were trying to starve her to death, but the chick keeps holding on."

Nate couldn't believe his ears. Wanting to hear more, he switched sides… pretending to adjust the other boot laces.

"Yep, but you know what happens first!"

"Oh yeah, the final party!"

Nate almost fell head first into the dirt! Dear God. He hoped that he misunderstood.

These morons are sicker than I thought, Nate thought...still stalling for time and more information.

"Man, even the big-wigs are coming for this one!" They continued.

"Mark your calendar, for the 30th."

Not able to stomach any more, Nate took off in a slow jog.

How could they do this? They weren't men, they were sick...sick animals! Nate knew that something had to be done, immediately. The truth was, he didn't know if she could hold on that long. Nate's mind began to race, then it hit him!

The urge to vomit! He leaned over into the dense bushes and puked his guts out.

Once finished, he sat for a moment with his back against the tree, replaying the conversation over and over in his mind. Each time he did, it ticked him off all over again! He was more determined than ever to get her out of there.

He immediately leapt to his feet and strode towards his tree.

He found it and climbed up as quickly as he could. Climbing took a little more effort this time due to the vomiting. By the time he reached the branch with his equipment, his energy was zapped. This time he had a small backpack on his back, which would enable him to carry more.

Not knowing what he might need, he packed some of everything into the bag. He also brought the remaining food that he had; a bag of chips, a pack of ration and two bottles of water.

Nate strapped on the backpack and reached for his phone in the duffle. Lou had provided him with a government-issued cell phone that was tapped into the satellite. It was guaranteed to never signal for as long as it was on the face of the earth. He dialed Lou's number and waited. He wasn't sure what time it was in the States, and he really didn't care! The phone rang and rang.

"Come on, Lou—pick up, man," Nate commanded telepathically.

Just when he was about to give up, Lou answered.

"Hello, my boy," he said groggily.

"Your boy, my behind! Lou, man, you are a dirty dog! You could have briefed me a little more! You could have at least prepared me for what I was walking into."

"How is she?" asked Lou.

"How is she?" mocked Nate sarcastically. "She's dying! She's slowly dying! It's their plan to kill her! The word is, they intend to have their way with her first! I'm talking about rape here, Lou.It's sick and it's evil! I promise you, she won't survive it! I don't have time to fill you in with all the details. I need assistance, ASAP!"

"Tell me what you need. You tell me what, when and where and I'll get it there," Lou assured him. They quickly implemented a plan and place of delivery.

Nate made it back to the compound, with plenty of time left before his shift. The shifts had rotated and now Moose had nights. Nate was going to try to convince him to switch with him.

"Yo, Moose," he said as he entered the quarters. "Man, do you wanna switch with me? I got evenings this week, but I prefer nights...you know what I mean?"

"Yeah, yeah man...if you wanna switch, no problem with me. Heck, I got things that I want to do at night anyway, it's too hot during the day. I'm already dressed. In a few hours, I will go on in your place. I got you," said Moose.

Well, that was easier than I thought it would have been, thought Nate to himself, as he laid across his bed for a well-needed nap.

When Nate arrived on the third floor for his shift, there wasn't a soul in sight.

Where is he, thought Nate. Observing the room, he saw Moose's lunch bag and watch on his desk.

Wait! I know better, Nate realized, throwing his things onto his desk and heading toward the girl's door. At that very moment, her door swung open and Moose came out, buttoning his shirt.

It literally took everything Nate had within him not to snap his neck!

Trying to keep his composure, he quickly turned away, walked over to his desk and leaned on it while Moose gathered his things.

"So, umm, tell me—you... are partying again...?"

Nate walked over to the water cooler. He desperately needed a drink.

He hated being fake in front of these morons!

Moose sensed the aggravation in Nate's voice. He

thought that the wisest thing to do would be not to answer the question.

Man, if I wasn't saved…I'd kill this one right now, thought Nate.

Then he repented for the thought.

"God help me," Nate mumbled under his breath.

His military training had taught him not to let his face reveal his thoughts.

He was really grateful for it, because at the moment, he felt the need to puke and to kick somebody's behind! He mentally blocked Moose out as he went on and on talking.

"OK, guess I will go up and get a shower and a nap. She's in there, in case you change your mind," said Moose, exiting the room.

"I won't," growled Nate.

Moose turned around to make one more comment, but Nate intercepted before he could get the words out.

"Man, just get the heck out of here!" Nate snapped.

He quickly caught the tone that he was using and tried to fix it.

"I mean dang, man, you just worked a full shift. What are you trying to do, hang around and work mine too? You can't make all the money!"

Moose stood there perplexed for a moment. Then he gave a fake laugh and made an exit for the second floor. He wasn't quite sure what had happened. But the one thing he knew for sure, was that he didn't want to tick off Nate.

As soon as he left, Nate went into his drawer and grabbed the backpack and the keys to her door. He sat patiently on top of his desk, trying to allow Moose time to get settled upstairs. About twenty minutes went by and Nate couldn't hold out any longer.

Pulling on his skull cap, he marched towards the door. As he got closer he heard it. Total silence! No moans, no whimpers, nothing.

"Oh, my God," said Nate, as his fidgety hands struggled to get the key in the door.

As always, he was never in too much of a rush to send up a quick prayer…

"Oh Lord, please don't let her be dead. Give me the strength to do whatever it is that I need to do. I know that it was you that brought me here. Amen."

He took a deep breath, turned the lock and pushed the door open. It seemed as if the disgusting odor had gotten worse. He took out his mini flashlight and began to tread through the stench of feces and filth. Not knowing what he was going to find, Nate's nerves were on the edge. He could feel his heart pounding in his chest and he had the worst case of butterflies, ever.

Wow, there she was: same position, chained to the old, dirty bed. She had lost even more weight and her skin was filthy. She was so weak this time, she didn't even hear him at all.

Nate walked up to the foot of the bed and gave the dirty mattress a nudge with his knee. Slowly, she opened her eyes. She raised her head high enough to see another man standing before her. Exhausted, with no fight left, she rolled over in surrender, offering herself to him. Nate nudged the bed again, never leaving his position. When she raised up, he shook his head no. She squinted her eyes, trying to see more clearly. Then he gave her the eye signal.

It was him, he came back! The green-eyed angel! She collapsed onto the bed with relief. Nate threw the backpack off, on to the bed and moved to her side.

She could barely keep her eyes open. However, the calmness that overcame her face let him know that she recognized him. He lightly stroked her matted head.

Her hair hadn't been washed or combed in so long, it was a dirty, matted mess.

Those idiots just didn't know when to stop. What kind of man in his right mind would do this, Nate asked himself. With no time to waste, he squatted down by the bed, said another quick prayer and got started. She was in such bad shape he didn't know where to begin. He grabbed the remainder of the dried herbs and dropped it into the bottle of water. Then, he took his pocket knife and punched a hole into the Capri Sun. She laid there like a helpless baby bird with her mouth open, as he squeezed it into her mouth.

She was so thirsty! Ripping open the pack of ration, he found a small tube of peanut butter. Although it was a little thick, Nate knew that she needed the protein.

She was so hungry, it didn't take as long as he'd expected for her to finish the whole tube. Nate rinsed it down with the herbal water. Surely, it wasn't the best tasting thing that she'd ever drank, but when you're parched, you are grateful for anything. Fighting for her every breath of life, she managed to give Nate a semi-smile...trying to say thank you.

This time it had to be a quick in and out visit. The guys weren't asleep, and Nate couldn't risk getting caught. He fed her, cleaned her up as best as he could, gathered all the trash/evidence and aimed for a timely departure. She sat and watched him sadly. She didn't want him to leave, but she had a feeling that he'd be back!

Before he left, he gave her the eye signal. She managed to give him a small smile, then rolled over, turning her back as he walked away. Nate felt like someone had just sucker punched him in the heart! Regardless of the risk, he knew that he needed to make an emergency trip to the tree! He locked her door and continued right out the back door.

Once outside again he ran like a mad man. It didn't matter that it was dark, he'd memorized the terrain. All he could think about was getting in touch with Lou.

He didn't even remember climbing the tree, getting the phone or auto-dialing the number. He was snapped back into reality at the sound of Lou's voice.

This time Lou answered on the second ring.

"Nate, Nate, what's going on?"

"Change of plans, bro, she's sinking fast! We need help and we need it now! I mean, like, in two days, max!"

"Shoot, tell me what you need..."

"One! Enough food, ration, and water for about 2 weeks. She's going to need hers to be for a liquid diet.

"Two! Enough clothes for a couple of months for both of us... at least until we can get on our feet. Sundresses for a petite woman will do fine."

"Go on, I feel it coming," said Lou.

"Three! Five grand in unmarked bills, cell phones that are untraceable."

"Anything else?" asked Lou.

"Yes," laughed Nate. "Four! I need transportation. I'm talking about a state of the art Hummer!

Super edition. But I need it to look plain, so that it can blend in...no distractions. The inside needs to have only the two front seats. The back, empty with seatbelts built into the floor. She also must have excellent climbing power! There's a lot of rugged terrain out here. I'm talking about Marine surplus on steroids!"

"Got it," said Lou.

"Anything else?" interrupted Lou.

"Yeah," said Nate, "I need it ASAP! The plan is to train until Wednesday, Thursday night...we need to get out of here!"

"Where do you want me to put all of this, if possible?" asked Lou.

"Not if it is possible; make it possible," commanded Nate.

"Okay, man, you got it…now tell me where?"

"I have found a clearing about a mile and a half away from the compound. I have already tracked the coordinates and will send them to you shortly. Lou, in a bag…I'll need a pair of high-tech night goggles, Pedialyte, sports drinks and some medical supplies. Chief, need any and everything that you can think of… a hospital in a bag!"

"Well, I have my work cut out for me, but I will have it all in place by midnight Wednesday," said Lou.

"Good, I figured we'd leave around 2 a.m.…by 6 a.m. we would be long gone!"

"Won't they try to hunt you down?"

"Probably, and speaking of hunting…I will have some toys, right?"

"Locked and loaded," laughed Lou.

"Passports?"

"I'll have them made and put in the dash of the hummer. I have her picture in the computer, it won't be a problem. I knew that you were the man for this job," chuckled Lou. I'll text you when everything is in place, you know the code."

"Now go back to bed, to your wife," laughed Nate.

He returned to the compound just as quietly and swiftly as he'd left. He finished out his shift with peace in his heart: "change was coming"!

Nate didn't get to bed until about noon. He spent

the morning scoping and mapping his path. He knew everything had to be perfect, no time for slip-ups or mistakes.

Using his machete, Nate went through the jungle scoring trees. He marked some at the bottom, the middle and the top. The marks would keep him on course, on escape night. They would be fresh enough for him to see; yet undetectable by anyone else.

The plan seemed to be coming together. Now, all he had to do was to pull it off!

He prayed that she would be strong enough to survive it. The next few nights, Nate took a run while he was on duty. He waited until he was sure that everyone was asleep, using the flashlight on his hat; he practiced. He was trying to get even more familiar with the path in the dark. Soon, he wouldn't be running alone.

Carrying a duffle bag filled with coconuts strapped to his back, Nate ran. He practiced as if his life depended on it, which it did.

His tree food supply was gone. So Nate would pack a little extra food in his lunch from the quarters upstairs. Fruit, water, coconut milk, etc., whatever he could find that would keep her hydrated, until it was time to make their move.

During the day, he increased his workout routine, which did not go unnoticed. He knew that his roommates were watching him. They just thought that he was some fitness geek. Little did they know there was a master plan, predestined by the Master above.

Physically, Nate felt ready; he only hoped that he was as mentally and emotionally prepared.

CHAPTER THREE

Thursday finally arrived. Nate had been anxious all day. Midnight Wednesday night, Nate received his confirmation text from Lou. "Everything's a go."

Relieved to know that everything was in place, Nate spent most of the day getting his mind prepared and praying in the spirit. Now, the only thing that he could do was wait.

He'd visited the tree earlier, taken everything stuffed it into the duffle bag and hid it in a bush right outside the front door of the compound. He took the onesie, baby carrier, Gatorade and night goggles and stuffed them into his backpack.

Nate's shift started at 8:00 on Thursdays, another reason why he'd chosen this night. When he arrived, he was relieved to find no one coming out of her room. He tried his best to remain cool, calm and collected… just like any other night.

Nate got off the elevator and once again, the silence pierced his heart. Dear God, I hope she is still alive, he thought, as he took his position at his desk. He'd overheard the guys planning on staying up, playing cards and getting a little drunk, since neither one was on patrol.

Man, of all nights, said Nate to himself! Well, I guess that knocks out our 2 a.m. departure! He began to brainstorm for a plan B.

Sitting quietly at his desk, he watched them plan and chat before leaving for upstairs. Moose high-fived him on the way out.

"Adios and good riddance!" mumbled Nate to himself as he left.

The party upstairs started immediately, they didn't waste any time!

Nate sat there patiently listening, as they yelled, laughed and slammed things around. There were only two of them up there, but it sounded like fifty people.

About three o'clock the party slowed down; the yelling, cursing and slamming ceased.

I guess that means that they are asleep now...I'd better give them a few more minutes to make sure they are completely knocked out, he thought.

He unlocked his bottom drawer, took out a pair of running shoes and his long sleeve running shirt. He put them on and left the uniform shirt and boots on the top of the desk as a souvenir for his co-workers to find in the morning.

It was now 3:30 a.m...seemed like the drunkards were out!

Nate was ready. He could feel the adrenaline begin to pump through his veins. It was time to make his move. He knew that he only had 30 minutes to get her dressed: 4:00 a.m. was "Game Time"!

He grabbed his backpack and headed for her door. Although he was pushed for time, he still took time to pray… Father God, please let her be alive, give her what she needs to hold on, until I can get her to safety. Father, touch my mind, feet, legs, and body. Give me the strength to be swift, strong and the ability to carry out this mission...Amen.

Nate slipped his ski mask on and entered the room.

The stench almost stopped his breath. It also seemed as if the rodents had multiplied. Moving as fast as he could in the semi-darkness, he raced towards the bed, holding his breath.

"I'm coming, babe, hold on!"

There she was, curled in the fetal position again.

She was so weak, when he rolled her over she fell backwards like a sack of potatoes. She was giving up the fight!

Nate placed the bag on the bed and gave her a little nudge. She could barely open her eyes. He wasn't sure if she even recognized him; but at this point it really didn't matter...time was ticking!

Nate unzipped the bag and began to dress her, putting on the Depends and onesie. Then, he reached for the baby carrier and threw it on the bed. Lou came through! It was super durable, made from parachute material. He tried to give her a few sips of water, using the bottle top as a cup. Poor thing, she was too weak to take a sip. Nate used the cup and poured little capfuls into her mouth; enough to wet her pallet.

Time was of the essence!!!

Realizing someone was touching her, she forced open her eyes for as long as she could. Nate gave her the eye signal and put one finger to his lips, saying "shhh".

She knew...she somehow understood that the time had come for him to rescue her. It was confirmed by the look on her face. Nate zipped her in, picked her up like a baby and strapped her to his back. Then, he grabbed his night goggles and pulled them onto his face. He double-checked the buckles and straps in front of him, making sure that they were securing her to his back. Then he sprang into action!

Lou had the measurement and proportions to the "T"!

Everything was perfect. He didn't have to worry about dragging her or injuring her on the run. The hoodie was big enough to fit over both of their heads and her arms were tucked in.

Showtime, thought Nate as he strode towards the door.

The office was completely silent, which meant that they were up there fast asleep.

Throwing his backpack and the shackle keys on the desk as another token of his victory, Nate saluted and made his exit.

Nope, no elevator tonight. Better take the stairs, he figured. She was about 100 lbs dripping wet; Nate conquered the stairs with ease. The exit put him out at the front of the compound which was barely used.

A glimpse at his watch told him they were on track: it was 4:00 on the dot. Nate grabbed the bag out of the bush, slipped his head through the straps and began to run.

"Come on, Jesus," he said aloud as he flipped on the night goggles. They were the top of the line as well. It was as if he were running in the daytime.

Moving like a mighty panther, Nate strode through the jungle, looking for his marked trees to keep him on route. With the path memorized, he arrived at the halfway mark fast. The jilting of each step made the precious cargo on his back moan and groan. It sounded like music to his ears, confirming that she was still alive. For the first time, he found himself smiling at the sound of her whimpers. They reassured him that he did the right thing.

As Nate ran, dodging the bushes, he kept glancing at his watch. He was determined to leave before 5:00 a.m., knowing that at 6:00 am they'd realize that she was missing. He wanted to get at least an hour of time between them. In fact, he wanted to be completely out of their territory. With that thought in mind, Nate pressed in harder. His adrenaline was pumping a mile a minute. I should be there soon, he said to himself. Suddenly, it was as though his heart jumped into his throat—Yes, there it was, the banana tree that he'd chopped in half, his last sign!

"Hold on baby, we are almost there," he said.

Like most experienced runners, he gave the last leg of the race his all.

Just as he exited the jungle, there she was, sitting there in the clearing, waiting just as Lou had promised.

"Thank you, Jesus," said Nate out loud.

Stopping to observe his surroundings, he paused before moving towards the vehicle. He wanted to make sure that the coast was clear. The last thing that he needed was company; especially with her on his back. Slowly yet carefully, Nate moved in towards the Hummer. It looked like a beat-up piece of junk, just like he'd ordered.

Nate pressed his fingers underneath the door handle. She immediately unlocked, and Nate opened the door.

As ordered, the rear of the Hummer was empty with floor straps. He quickly turned around and backed into the vehicle, letting her down slowly, until her frail body was lying on the floor. Pressed for time, he didn't have time to take her out of the gear, so he buckled her in and proceeded.

He thought that he would try to give her a couple more sips of water before they got on the road.

"Come on baby, drink something for me," he thought, as he tried to force a little water into her.

She was so out of it, she couldn't take much. Nate shut the doors and made a dash to the driver's side. He plopped himself down into the seat and reached for the ignition keys...only to find they weren't there!

What? No keys? Nate began to search.
Glove compartment...Nope!

Underneath the seat...Nope!

Over the sun visor.... Nope! Frustration began to set in." Come on, Lou! I know he didn't forget the keys!" Nate thought. Glancing at his watch, he realized it was 4:50 a.m. They really needed to get out of there!

Nate stopped, sat back in his seat and took a deep breath.

"OK Lord, where are the keys?" he said in a silent prayer.

He heard as clear as a bell, "How did you get in there?"

"My fingerprints," Nate realized in response.

He immediately sprang up in his seat. Knowing that the ignition switch wasn't big enough for all his fingers, he tried his thumb. When Nate pressed the ignition, the old gal began to purr! She would only start by his thumbprint! "Lou, Lou, Lou," he said, smiling now.

The sound of the engine brought tears to his eyes. He raised both his hands in a moment of praise. "Thank you, Father," he said as he drove off.

"OK lil lady, let's get the heck out of here," said Nate, glancing back over his shoulder to make that sure she was okay. On his run a few days earlier, he'd found a back road that led away from the compound. It looked like it hadn't been driven in years, but it would have to do. Nate was confident in the fact that Lou had sent him a Hummer that could handle the roughest terrain. The road was rough, but the Hummer took the beating well.

The precious cargo, on the other hand, bounced around on the floor moaning, and groaning. She wasn't enjoying the ride. After about an hour of bouncing his brains out, Nate finally reached the main road. Lou had left a map for him with coordinates of how to get to Milo, the next town. He plugged it into the GPS and they were on their way. Nate drove as quickly and safely as possible! He knew that she would need water soon, but he had no plans of stopping in Milo.

It was too dangerous. Surely these goons had contacts and now that their only payment from a tremendous debt was gone, they were going to be furious!

The logical thing to do was to keep it moving. By daybreak, Nate was pulling into the next town of Lares. According to the GPS, he had successfully put 300 miles between them.

Man, I'd love to see the looks on their faces when they realize that we aren't there, thought Nate, smiling. Glancing back to look at her, he noticed that she was pale. It was past time that he tended to her. He began to look for a safe place to park. He spotted a clearance off the road and parked behind the big oak tree. Nate left the car running for the much-needed AC. He swung the doors open to find her lying there just as he'd left her, except she was sweating.

Man, I got to get her hydrated, thought Nate as he stripped her of the traveling gear. She definitely did not need to be sweating. He worked as fast as he could. He took her out of the gear and onesie, then into a cool sundress Lou had provided. Taking a cold bottle of water out of the cooler, he poured some into his hand and gave her face a light spray. She slowly opened her eyes and her mouth.

He began to stroke her head. This time, she opened her eyes wide and stared at him. It was the first time that she'd see him without the mask. Too weak to focus, she closed them again and began to drift out of consciousness. Nate frantically began to search for a vein on her legs, arms, all over her frail, dirty body; anywhere for one strong enough to sustain a needle. Desperately, he searched between the burns. She was so dehydrated, it was nearly impossible to find one. Finally, he found one one the sole of her foot.

She moaned as he stuck her foot and started the IV. Once again, old Lou came through. Just as he'd asked, the medicine bag was a mini hospital. It was stocked with everything and anything they thought that he could have possibly needed.

Nate hung the IV bag over the door, on the clothes hook. Then, he settled back on the floor, beside the cooler. He grabbed two sandwiches and a bottle of water—he was famished!

He hadn't even thought about eating and only stopped to use the bathroom twice. The only thing that he could think about was getting her to Chris.

Exhaustion overcame him quickly and when he woke up, it was an hour later. It had also been hours since shift change, things had to be chaos back at the compound! "Yes, baby, we are gone, see us in your dreams...'cause that's as close as you will ever get to us," laughed Nate. He was feeling proud about his decision to get her out when he did. He thanked God for the victory!

Once more he looked her over; she was resting, so he climbed over into the driver's seat.

She needed medical attention ASAP, the kind that he didn't have the skills to provide.

Nate had already contacted a doctor. His old high school classmate and childhood friend Chris, who lived in San Cristobal. Nate informed him of the situation and Chris promised to be waiting for their arrival. Time went by quickly and before he knew it, Nate was at the foothills. Chris personally met him as promised and escorted them up to his guesthouse in the hills.

Nate got out, looking around and scoping out the territory.

"Don't worry, you will be safe here, I promise," Chris assured him. They quickly gave an old school dap and proceeded to get her out of the vehicle. Chris reached to open the door, but Nate intercepted.

"I got her!" Guarding her like she was his property, he took her childlike body out of the truck and carried her in his arms into the guesthouse. Chris had an office and practice in the back.

Nate laid her down on the hospital bed and stepped back. Chris and his staff immediately began to work with her. "Her pulse is very weak; Sheena, call the specialists in!" yelled Chris.

"Well, my friend, you did save her! She never

would have made it without that IV! But I need to move it, this vein has blown." As soon as Chris removed the needle, she began to seize. With his hand over his mouth in disbelief, Nate stepped further back, out of the way. He felt so helpless; this time there was nothing that he could do to help her. Noticing the hurt in Nate's face, Chris yelled, "Somebody get him out of here!"

One of the nurses took Nate out of the room into the hall. The only thing he could hear was Chris shouting orders and people running. Nate's legs began to buckle, and he decided it would be best if he sat down. Sitting there, with his back against the wall, he did the only thing that he knew…he prayed.

When Chris pushed the door open, Nate sprang to his feet.

"Is she—?" he demanded.

"No, no—she's alive—barely! But I must tell you," Chris replied, "I had to put her in an induced coma."

"What?"

"She's been through so much, she needs the rest. Now, only time will tell.

All I can say is that I hope that you aren't too attached! We will know more in the next 24-48 hours. Honestly, it doesn't look good; but I believe she's a fighter."

"Man! Man, OK…do you have anything to drink?" asked Nate, rubbing his head as he tried to process the situation.

"You don't drink," Chris responded.

"Man, my nerves…"

"Say no more, follow me."

Chris led him into another office, where he walked over to the desk and pulled a bottle of wine out of the drawer. Nate bucked his eyes, in dismay.

"Old Christmas present," explained Chris, as he poured some into a bathroom paper cup. "I apologize for the crystal glasses," he said, trying to lighten the mood. He was worried about his friend.

"Man, right now, I don't even care!" replied Nate as he took a couple of sips, before throwing it all down.

"Can I see her?" he asked.

"How about we let her rest for an hour or two, then you can see her," suggested Chris.

Nate gave him a stern look.

"She's in good hands. Trust me and let her rest awhile. Plus, it'll give us a little time to get caught up. You can start by telling me what the heck happened to her."

"Huh, where do I begin?" mused Nate.

He started telling him the story from the beginning, as they walked out onto the porch and took a seat. Time passed quickly as Nate filled Chris in on the situation.

Suddenly, out of nowhere, Nate stopped mid-sentence and blurted, "Can I see her now?"

It was more than obvious that his mind had never left her.

"Sure, I will walk with you."

Nate stopped and took a deep breath before entering the room. The nurses were still standing around her bed, having just finished bathing her and cleaning her wounds. There she laid in her hospital gown, looking awful.

"What in the world happened to this woman?" one of the nurses asked.

Nate dodged the question by asking, "How is she?"

Then, "OMG, what happened to her hair?"

He had just noticed that they shaved all her hair off!

Linda, the head nurse, spoke up. "We had to shave it all, mister...she had an infestation of bugs in her hair. We needed to treat her scalp!

Her blood pressure is coming up, but she is still very weak and barely hanging onto life."

"Can I have a moment alone with her?" asked Nate.

"What? No sir, are you crazy?"

"It's OK...it's fine," said Chris, "he didn't do this."

They all exited the room and Nate just stood there for a moment, looking at her frail body. Then, he pulled up Chris' stool, sat beside her and took her hand in his.

How could someone do this to another human being, he wondered.

Of course, being military he'd seen torture, but

most of those were bad people; they had it coming! This was an innocent, probably vibrant young woman that didn't have a choice!

He began to talk to her.

"First of all, I hope that you can hear me? I would like to say that I'm sorry. I'm sorry for everything that those animals did to you. I'm sorry that I didn't get there sooner, but that was kinda out of my control. To be honest with you, I didn't even want to take this mission. My lieutenant convinced me to do it. He said that I was the only man for the job. The first time that I laid eyes on you, I knew that it was God who sent me to do the job! I knew that he sent me to get you out of there!"

Stroking her hand as he spoke, he began to change his focus and speak to God.

"OK, Lord, mission accomplished; that is, through your strength and wisdom. Now it's your turn, there is nothing else that I can do. Please don't let her die; she has already suffered so much!" Tears began to flow. "Please, don't let her die for the sins of her father," he pleaded. "Lord, give her the strength to fight."

Feeling physically, emotionally and spiritually drained, he laid his head down beside her and continued to pray in the spirit. He didn't know that she heard every word that he said. Weak and frail, she so desperately wanted to respond to him, but she couldn't.

She was so moved when she heard his voice!

"He's speaking! He finally speaks, and when he does...he's praying for me!

A woman that he doesn't even know! I wish that I could tell him that I can hear him."

With nowhere else to turn, in her comatose mind, she too began to talk to God.

"God, I don't know you," she thought. "I have always been taught that you weren't real.

"But he believes...this man believes in you and he's crying for me. He cared and protected me, when my own family wouldn't. He says it was you, who sent him to get me! I just want to tell him thank you and that I can hear him; but I can't. I want to believe too. God, if you are real, please help me...I have nothing left," she pleaded.

Then, she heard a small voice saying, "I am real!"

"Then I believe," she thought.

"Just as I heard his prayer; I also have heard yours...trust and believe! Now wake up and go back to him, touch his head." Stepping out on a mustard seed of faith, she lifted her frail hand. It felt as if it weighed a ton, but she placed it on the back of his head.

At this point, Nate's face was buried in his arms and he was deep into prayer. Her hand was so light that Nate didn't even realize that it was there. As she came around, she began to whimper. Now that got his attention! He could recognize that whimper anywhere. Immediately, he regained focus, took her hand from his head and began to yell for help! Chris and his nurse came running through the door.

"What? What's wrong?"

"She is coming around—she touched me, and she has been crying…"

"She's not crying now, and you are holding her hand," Chris pointed out sarcastically.

"Trust me, I know her cry!" Nate snapped. "Come on man, I'm not crazy…I'm telling you, it happened! Check her, check her please…" he pleaded.

Chris began to check her vitals again.

Meanwhile, Nate began to tap the back of her hand, while giving her a little pep talk.

"Come on, girl, I know you can hear me, wake up!"

Tap, tap! Nate hit her hand…

Again…tap, tap!

Suddenly, she gave a low moan and Nate could feel a bit of resistance.

"Yes ma'am, come on, fight…fight! Look Chris, I told you!" said Nate, constantly smacking her hand.

"Nate, take it easy," said Chris.

"Nope, nope…she feels it and she doesn't like it! She's coming around…"

Smack, smack! His taps got harder and harder.

The moans began to get stronger and louder!

Then came forth a groggy Latina voice, strained as if from laryngitis, "Ay…ay, ay Papi, please stop hitting me!"

Nate threw his head back, laughing with joy and relief. He placed her hand down on the bed and threw up his hands in surrender.

"OK, OK—you're talking; I'm stopping," he said, smiling.

"Mm...hello, green eyes," she murmured as she slowly opened her eyes.

"Well hello, ma'am," Nate replied, smiling.

"Wow, it's a wonder what a day of antibiotics and rest will do!" observed Chris.

"What's your name, honey?" Linda chimed in.

"Silvia," whispered the patient.

"OK Silvia, do you know where you are?"

"Nope, all I know is I'm with green eyes, he got me out!"

Nate threw up his hands unto the Lord in praise!

He felt like crying again, but this time decided to man up.

Nurse Linda gave her a few more sips of water to moisten her dry throat.

"Silvia, I'm Dr. Chris and I'm here to help you. Do you remember anything?"

"I remember being in that filthy place and green eyes…he took me away from those

bad people."

"Good, that's right!" exclaimed Chris. "Now, you are at my house and clinic. Don't worry, we're going to take good care of you.

This is my other nurse, Constance; call her if you need anything, OK?"

Silvia nodded. Still weak and tired, she drifted in and out of consciousness.

"Well, everything seems fine," said Chris, turning

to Nate. "Her BP is coming up, pulse is normal, breathing and oxygen levels are coming up!"

"I'd say it was a miracle," said Nate.

"Indeed," Chris replied.

"Well my friend, I think she's back. Now, she just needs to regain her strength. We'll leave the two of you alone for a minute. Then, I want you to let her get some rest."

Nate nodded.

"Holla if you need us," said Chris

"I will, and thanks so much, man," said Nate, giving his former classmate a big hug.

"Ha, man, let go, you're being too sentimental...not in front of the ladies," joked Chris.

Nate gave him a big shove, then Chris and Constance left the room.

Nurse Linda updated her charts, then she left as well.

Nate walked back over to Silvia's bedside and extended his hand.

"I think I should formally introduce myself...hello, I am Nate, a.k.a. green eyes."

She smiled, extending her hand weakly.

"Hello, green eyes, my name is Silvia."

Goodness Silvia, for a couple that just met, we have been through some things!"

They both laughed.

"Do you know that you're a miracle? I thought that—I thought that I'd lost you. I was..."

"Praying for me..." she interrupted.

Nate stood in awe. "You heard me?"

"Loud and clear," she said. "I don't know what happened, but I know it was God! When I heard your voice for the first time, you were praying for me; a woman that you didn't even know. I couldn't believe it! I was raised to believe that God wasn't real. I really wanted you to know that I could hear you. I even heard you crying."

Nate blushed.

"So I asked God in my mind if he was real," Silvia continued. "If he was real, I asked him to let me give you a sign, so that you would know that I heard you. That's when I heard his voice."

"Whose voice?" asked Nate.

"God's," she replied. "He told me that he was real. He said to trust and believe and to come back to you! I felt warm, then he gave me strength to reach out and touch you. All I can say is…I know God is real; now I believe!"

"Oh, taste and see that the Lord is good," said Nate.

"Huh?"

"Nothing, don't worry about it right now, I will teach you later," he said.

"OK, I will be around," she said, smiling.

"Go to sleep now, I'll be over here in the chair." Refusing to leave her side, Nate sat in the corner and praised God, as she drifted back to sleep.

"Thank you, Father; it's only a matter of time before she gets saved."

Four weeks went by and Silvia grew stronger each day. Her hair was beginning to grow back, she'd gained a little weight, her curves were coming in and her skin was beginning to heal. The deep burns were now peeling craters.

Nate could see what could have piqued the kingpin's interest. She was long waisted, with hips, curves and thighs that even her frailness couldn't hide. A few months ago, she must have been stunning!

She came into the kitchen while Nate and Chris were having breakfast. Nate had to keep refocusing his attention, in order to stay engaged in the conversation.

"Ah, I see," said Chris with meaning.

"You see what?" asked Nate.

"I think someone has caught your eye and maybe even your heart."

"Naw," said Nate, blushing.

"That's funny, your mouth is saying no, but your face is saying yes…" said Chris, laughing. "You can't keep your eyes off her."

"Why don't you just stick to doctoring?" snapped Nate sarcastically. "No, but seriously, Chris, I don't even understand the connection; ever since the moment I met her, I've felt this need to protect her."

"Where do you plan on going when you leave here?" Chris asked.

"I'm working on that, but I can promise you wherever it is, she will be going with me."

"Are you sure about that?"

"Nope, but I'm hoping…" Nate confessed. "By

the way, when do you think she will be strong enough to leave?"

"Give her another week," suggested Chris.

"I guess…I will use this week to map out a plan."

As he'd stated, Nate used the week to implement a plan.

Silvia was thriving and making friends amongst them. Nate silently watched as she and a few nurses sat at the picnic table under the big oak tree.

He truly hated to interrupt their girl time, but they really needed to talk.

Before he could plan anything else, he needed to know if he would be traveling alone. Well, now is as good of a time as any, he thought.

Making his way over to the women, he politely asked Silvia to take a walk with him.

"Well, let me see how I am going to say this," Nate began. "Silvia, you know that my mission is over. Actually, my whole career is over. Your family is gone, and it is time that I returned to normal life. I guess my question to you is, what do you want to do? This seems to be safe, but we both know that we can't stay here forever. Although we haven't seen any of them, our enemies are still a little too close. Do you want to go with me?" he asked.

"Yes, I know that I can't stay here. As far as my family goes…all of them are dead to me!

I have no one! No one but you; the man that saved me."

"No, no; now, I am the man that rescued

you...only God can save you," Nate pointed out.

Realizing that she was still just coming into faith, he didn't try to explain...he just continued.

"So, does this mean that you are going with me?"

"Yes, it does. Where are we going? I guess it really doesn't matter. I will follow those green eyes to the ends of the earth!" she replied.

Trying not to make it obvious, Nate gave a quick sigh of relief.

He really couldn't imagine leaving her. "OK then, I will tell you now, we will be leaving the country," he told her.

"But wait...I don't have a passport or anything. How can I get out of the country, and what about immigration?"

Nate chuckled, "Trust me, you have a passport and everything else that you will need; you just haven't seen them yet."

"Oh, so you just knew that I was going to say yes, huh?" questioned Silvia.

"Well...I was hoping you would, but in my world, there is always a plan B."

"What was your plan B?"

"How did you get here?" he asked.

"Passed out in your arms."

"And there you have it. If you had to be passed out or carried out kicking and screaming...you were going!"

"Nate!" she exclaimed, in disbelief.

"Well...I've worked and prayed too hard to leave

you behind! Besides, I never want to have to wonder if those goons ever found you. I want to make sure that they NEVER touch you again! The best way to do that is to have you with me!"

"Aww, thank you…I'm beginning to see that behind all of that buff, you are a big teddy bear!"

"Shh, that's top-secret information!" laughed Nate.

"When do we leave?"

"Soon, but first let's make sure you have fully recovered. I will have Chris check you out. Meanwhile, we will start some light PT at 6 a.m. It will help you to build up your strength."

"What, ahh really, Papi? I don't like to exercise!" protested Silvia, her hands on her hips.

There it was, that Latino flair! He thought it was so cute!

"Well missy, you have to. We never know what type of situation we could encounter.

I want to make sure that you are physically strong enough to hold your own, to at least run! So, PT and a li'l defensive training starting ASAP, tomorrow…got it?"

"Got it," said Silvia.

"Great! Now that we have that settled, I need to finalize a few more things so that we can get out of here."

"OK," she said, smiling as she went back to join the others.

Now that he had the situation taken care of, there

was only one more left.

Once again, he would need Lou.

"Lou?"

"Nate!"

"Yeah, it's me," he replied. "Well, we made it! She's OK, coming around…almost lost her, but everything is fine."

"Good! Are you ready to bring her in? It's been a few weeks and I'm starting to feel a little heat."

Nate ignored the question.

"First of all…did you keep your promise?"

"Yes sir, I did, and you are officially out! You have a clean slate!"

"Thanks, Lou," said Nate."Now, I have two more favors…"

"Shoot," said Lou.

"Well, the first one concerns Mama Joyce."

"Oh, she's safe. I had her put in one of our safe houses the day that you started the mission.

Yeah, she's fine…worried about you, of course," laughed Lou. "Bring it on, man! I can feel something coming!"

"OK, I will shoot straight from the hip. So, you say that I'm done, right? I'm completely out. Now my question for you is, can you look away?"

"What do you mean?"

"I meant just that: can you look away? I'm gone!"

"You know that they still want to question her, right?"

"No," said Nate. "She's been through enough,

now just answer the question!"

"This…coming from the man who rushed into a burning house to save my only daughter?

Yes, yes, my friend, I can look away…don't worry about anything!"

An overwhelming relief came over Nate and he settled back in his chair.

"OK…well then, these are the two other things. I need the Hummer delivered somewhere, and I want my momma!"

"Just tell me when and where. Now, you know that Mama Joyce is like a real mother to me. This package I will be personally delivering," said Lou.

Nate told him what airport and time to have Mama Joyce there.

"As for the Hummer, I can have her on any location in two weeks," added Lou.

"OK then, two weeks it is; I will see you soon," replied Nate.

It was now the end of the week. Silvia was feeling good and Nate was comfortable about leaving.

"Well, that's about it," said Nate as he threw the last few things into the back of the Hummer.

"Man, Chris, I can't thank you enough."

Nate and Chris hugged as if they would never see each other again.

Silvia also hugged Chris. "Thank you for saving me," she said, trying to hold back the tears. Then, she corrected herself. "Well, I guess I should say thank you

for resuscitating me. Nate says only Jesus can save me."
She turned to Nate and said, "OK, I'm ready."

"Ready for what?" asked Nate.

"I'm ready to do what I need to, so that Jesus can save me. I don't know all of it, but I have been watching Christian TV. I heard him for myself and I know that he is real... I want to be like you, I want to be saved," Silvia said simply.

Nate was speechless at first. Just as he began to speak, Chris interrupted.

"I want it too. I want to be saved. I have known you all my life. I have been watching you praying. I saw this woman and I know the condition she was in...she was on the verge of death! Only a higher power could have brought her back to life. I need Jesus, too."

Nate couldn't believe his ears. He was so full, he couldn't hold back the tears...all he could do was praise God!

He walked over to the back of the Hummer and pulled out his Bible. Just as he
was about to tell them about Romans 10:9 and salvation, Constance spoke up.

"Wait, what about me? Is it too late for me? I want to be saved too; I don't want to
be left behind. My grandma used to take us to church. I have always heard about Jesus, just have never met him."

"Well, you are going to meet him today!" Nate said.

By now, there wasn't a dry eye among them.

Nate knew within his heart that this was part of the mission. God used him to lead three lives to Christ. Heaven was rejoicing!

Nate passed his Bible around, letting each of them read the passage for themselves. As they repeated the sinners' prayer, they all shed tears of joy.

All of Heaven rejoiced!

CHAPTER FOUR

Once on the road, Nate and Silvia talked constantly. It was the beginning of their lives together. They shared stories from their childhoods. He filled her in on Mama Joyce, their relationship and what growing up was like. He grew up dirt poor. She, on the other hand, was born with the silver spoon and fork in her mouth!

However, none of that mattered now; it was all gone. Nate could see the pain in her eyes as she talked about it. She made it more than clear that he was her only family now.

Nate felt sorry for her, but as for himself, he was excited.

He was only hours away from seeing his mother. Soldier or not, he was a proud mama's boy! They were meeting Lou at the airport at 3:00.

As soon as they walked into the small airport, a voice rang out over the crowd.

"Nate, Nate! Over here!"

A short, chunky woman was jumping up and down, trying to get their attention.

For a split second, Nate felt as if he was 8 years

old again.

Nate ran over to her, picked her up and planted kisses on her face.

"Mama!"

"Put me down, silly boy! What did I tell you about picking me up? One of these days, you're going to hurt me!" She was kicking, fussing, smacking him and loving it, all at the same time.

The moment was bittersweet, as Silvia stood thinking about her mother. The mother that she would never see again. As Nate put his mom down, he realized that he'd left Silvia. Quickly, he turned around and ran back to get her. She was still standing there in the same spot that he'd left her.

Nate grabbed her hand and walked her over to introduce her to his mother.

"Mom, I would like to introduce somebody to you; this is my friend Silvia.

Silvia, this is my Mama Joyce."

Mama Joyce gave her a quick head to toe glance, then directed her attention to her son. She had the look of a mom whose son brought home some nasty girl!

The chill was real! Antarctica!

Nate felt it too. There was no way that Silvia could have missed it.

Actually, the way that she squeezed his hand confirmed it.

"Mama," began Nate, trying to melt the ice. "Mama, Silvia is going to be staying with us."

"That's nice," she replied insincerely. "OK son,

so where are we going?"

"It's a surprise, but I am pretty sure all of us are going to love it. Life as we know it is about to change. Now come on, ladies…we can't miss our flight." He quickly escorted them out to the private runway.

"Don't let her get to you; her bark is worse than her bite," Nate whispered into Silvia's ear. The other passengers had already boarded the nine-seater private jet. Both women were very nervous and of course, they both wanted to sit beside Nate.

He politely squeezed in between them.

"Wow, it's nice in here," commented Mama Joyce. "My Louie really knows how to send his mama away in style."

"How long is the flight?" asked Silvia.

"Five to six hours at the most. Why, are you scared?"

"What makes you think that?"

"Probably because my fingers are turning blue," laughed Nate.

"Oh sorry, yes," Silvia relaxed her grip on his hand. "It's my first time flying."

"Really, you will be fine," Nate reassured her.

The movie was on, the lights were dimmed, and the flight was going well until they

hit turbulence and the plane began to shake.

Immediately, Silvia threw her leg over Nate's and she was reaching frantically for his neck!

He grabbed her hand before she could grab his neck.

"Whoa, wait a minute," he said, trying not to laugh. "It's OK, we're safe. We aren't crashing, I promise...calm down," he said soothingly.

Trusting in his every word, she relaxed back into her seat.

He gently took her leg and placed it back on her side, giving her a little pat

of reassurance on the knee.

"Sorry about that," Silvia said ruefully.

"No problem, I was scared the first time I felt turbulence too."

"Please. You don't get scared!"

"Not true ma'am, I can recall an incident a few months ago that had me scared out of my mind."

She smiled.

Nate then took her hand and held it the rest of the flight.

Mama Joyce sat quietly observing. Who was this woman and what in the world happened to her, she wondered. Surely, she had to be a project! Nate could do better than that.

"Wait a minute," said Mama Joyce looking out of the window. "Are those kangaroos? Are we going to the land down under?"

"Kangaroos?" said Silvia, turning and looking out the window too.

"Yes ma'am, we are going to the land down under, and if you can see the kangaroos you might want to turn around—we will be landing soon."

"Where are we going?" asked Silvia.

"We are going off the grid, to a remote village called Kundana. You both will love it there!"

"I don't know," said Mama Joyce, folding her arms. "I don't care too much for hot weather or extreme heat!"

"Would you rather be in the States alone, without me and always looking over your shoulder?" Nate asked.

"Well, down under it is," Mama Joyce quickly agreed.

"Now that's my girl," said Nate, laughing. Then he laid his head on her shoulder for a second.

"Big ole baby," said Mama Joyce, as she ran her fingers through his curly hair.

"Yeah, well you spoiled me," Nate pointed out.

"You are right about that," laughed Mama Joyce.

Silvia just sat there in awe. It had been a long time since she'd seen this type of family interaction and love. It made her miss it.

But then, she thought, how could she miss what she'd never had. They sold her, for Pete's sake!

No one thought that she knew about it, but she did.

She heard the guys talking about it one night during their little visits. Just as she began to slip into her own thoughts and depression, she was snatched back into reality by the sound of screeching tires. The plane landed in an open field.

Silvia unfastened her seatbelt and leapt to her feet!

"Whew, si, Papi, let's go!"

She was too anxious to get off the plane. It was also in that moment that Nate realized how glad he was that she decided to come along. He only hoped that he'd gotten her away far enough, to keep her safe.

As they exited the plane, an old jalopy of a truck pulled up. "Ha, he's back! Welcome back!" Gladiator yelled, one of three Aborigine men running to meet Nate.

"Gladiator?" asked Mama Joyce.

"Yeah, it's my nickname. Just go with it," Nate whispered.

Mama Joyce and Silvia stood quietly while the guys reunited.

"Oh, fellows, this is my mom Joyce, and this is my…"

He didn't want to say that she was his sister, because he really was beginning to like her, and he wasn't ready to tell them the truth, just yet.

"This is my girlfriend, Silvia," he finished. She blushed as he grabbed her hand.

It was important to show them that she meant something to him. The Aborigines are loyal people who would give their lives for their family.

Silvia couldn't believe that he introduced her as his girlfriend. She knew what she looked like!

She didn't look like a monster anymore, but she was far from pretty. She looked nothing like she used to; for that reason, she stayed away from mirrors.

"Ladies, this is my friend, Uncle Lupe."

"Come, come let us get you home, the misses are waiting," he said, gesturing towards the old truck.

"Where will we sit?" asked Mama Joyce.

"On the back," whispered Nate. "Come on, you will be fine."

While the other two men gathered their bags and strapped them to the roof of the truck, Nate and Uncle Lupe helped the ladies into the back. Silvia settled into her spot, shoulder to shoulder with Nate.

The ride to the village was as bad as expected. It was hot, dusty and bumpy; there were times when even Nate wondered if the jalopy would make it. The driver made a sharp left, throwing Silvia's frail body into Nate's arms. She couldn't help but notice the firmness of his chest, the strength of his biceps and his hairy arms. He really was a gladiator! OMG, just my luck that I was passed out each time he carried me, she thought. She quickly tried to dismiss the thought and straighten back up. It was obvious what she was thinking, by the way she was blushing.

Nate picked it up loud and clear!

Trying not to blush himself, he helped her back into her spot and slipped his arm around her to anchor her down...all while continuing his conversation with Lupe.

However, nothing went unnoticed by Mama Joyce, who was watching every move. She couldn't wait until she had the chance to talk to her son and find out just who this straggler really was.

As they turned the corner, people were standing

on both sides of the driveway, shouting

"Gladiator!"

Nate waved as if he were in a parade. "The people seem friendly," said Silvia.

"They are, you'll love them," replied Nate.

"As you can see, we did some work to the place, Gladiator," said one of the men. "No one has lived there since you left. We tried to spruce it up a little bit for you. When we found out that you were bringing the misses; we decided to bring the outhouse a little bit closer."

"Outhouse?" exclaimed Mama Joyce frantically.

"Oh, don't worry ma'am, we cleaned all around it; no bushes, no snakes, nothing!"

"Snakes?" yelled Silvia.

Trying to avoid the evil eye he was getting from both women, Nate thought it would be the perfect time to change the subject and introduce them to his other friends.

"Now this guy was my right-hand man when I was here. He treated me like a brother; this is Dhunganda. His name means 'lightning'. Just like lightning, he is fast and strong," They both laughed as they pulled up to the little cottage. It was cute and quaint.

"Will there be enough room for all of us?" queried Mama Joyce.

"Oh yes, ma'am, it is quite large in the back," explained the driver, honking his horn.

Suddenly, the screen door flew open and six

women came out running, jumping and cheering.

"What?" said Nate.

"Oh yeah, the misses have been up all night. They have prepared a feast for you and your family. Welcome home, Gladiator!" said Dhunganda. "I hope you are hungry?"

"Always," replied Nate.

The women met them at the truck, some speaking in English, others in their native language.

Nate embraced them and then introduced his mom and Silvia.

One of them said, "Ohh no, not this one…she is too skinny and needs a lot of work."

Silvia dropped her head in shame and embarrassment.

"Hi, my name is Arkarma…I am Dhunganda's wife."

"He's the one that was driving that piece of a truck of ours". She reached over to kindly and gently lift Silvia's head. "Now, y'all come on in and freshen up. The others will be joining us shortly."

Nate still remembered the house and led Silvia to her room. He could feel her hand trembling in his. Once inside, she immediately flopped down on the bed, unable to hold back her tears.

Still holding her hand, Nate knelt before her.

"I'm so sorry she said that," he said.

"Nope, she's right. I am skinny and ugly and need a lot of work. How am I supposed to live the rest of my life like this? I can't even stand to look at myself in the mirror; yes, I've seen myself, and I look horrific. Look at me!" she said, showing Nate her arms and legs.

"I've never been so ugly! Let's face it, they won; I will forever be paying for my father's debt! Another thing: I appreciate it, but you can stop introducing me as your girlfriend.

It's embarrassing, and nobody believes it, anyway!"

"Silvia, stop it! I'm a grown man and I have the right to date whomever I please! On that note, I'm going to my room. If you need me, I will be across the hall. Dhunganda put your bag in the corner. Please, freshen up; we have people waiting," said Nate.

He shut the door with just enough force to let her know that he was upset.

Meanwhile, Arkarma gave Mama Joyce a tour of the house and showed her where she would be sleeping.

Nate needed a moment with his friends...it was time for the talk.

He quickly shaved, washed up, dressed and joined them in the kitchen. After telling Silvia's story and explaining the situation, they all understood her condition.

"Poor woman, no wonder she looks so bad," said Arkarma.

"Well, at least you know that she's safe," said Dhunganda.

"Yes, and we will do whatever it takes to make sure that she stays safe. Tell us what we need to do," said Uncle Lupe.

"I truly don't think they will find us, but then again that girl is the payment for a fifteen-year-old debt. They won't give up easily," said Nate. "First, we must beef up security around here! We need to put up a fence on the perimeter of the property. I think we should also move the dogs. We should all build new dog houses, relocating them to the entrance on everyone's property. They will make great alarms."

"OK, we will start cutting wood first thing in the morning. Now, go get those ladies…I'm starving!" said Lupe.

"I'll get them," laughed Nate.

After their last conversation, Nate hoped that Silvia had calmed down.

He approached the bedroom door to find it open and Silvia sitting on the bed with wet hair.

"What's going on?" asked Nate. "I see you found the water in the basin and washed your hair, but why aren't you dressed? We have people out there waiting for us."

"I have nothing cute to wear. I can't go out there like this, they already think I'm ugly,

poor and nasty."

"That is not true. Now get up and go over there and look in the dresser."

"For what, Papi? I have nothing."

"Go look in the drawer," Nate insisted, gesturing towards the dresser.

Reluctantly, Silvia went over and opened the top

drawer.

"Everything in there belongs to you," said Nate.

Immediately, a big blushing smile came across her face. The drawer was full of bras and lacey panties. I think I'm gonna need a little more than these, Papi," said Silvia, holding up a pair of lace panties.

"OK, maybe you should try another drawer," suggested Nate, trying to maintain his

composure and not blush.

Silvia began to open drawer after drawer. They were all filled with clothes just

for her. Skirts, shorts, tank tops, dresses...the works!

She ran around the bed and gave Nate a big hug, holding him tightly.

"Thank you, Nate. Thank you for everything!" Then, her tears began to flow.

Automatically, Nate reached out to console her, stroking the small of her back.

"I owe you my life," she said, still holding on.

"No, you owe me nothing. I know God sent me to get you out of there. Mission accomplished; nobody deserves to go through what you went through," said Nate, planting a small kiss on her forehead. "I think we have taken long enough. We have tired, hungry people waiting for us out there."

"OK then, just give me that sundress out of the other top drawer, behind you," she said, trying to untangle her wet hair.

Nate turned around, reached in the drawer and

grabbed the dress. Then he turned back around, only to find Silvia standing there with the dirty clothes on the floor.

Sweet Jesus, she's naked, realized Nate.

"OK, you hurry up and put that on, I'm going out here with the others." He threw the dress on the bed and made a fast exit. Cigarette burned body or not; a naked woman, is a naked woman. Oh yeah, she's getting too comfortable with me, he thought as he joined the others.

"Where is Silvia?" asked Mama Joyce.

"Here I am," replied Silvia. All eyes were on her, as she came hurrying down the hallway barefooted, with the sundress on and bandana around her head.

"We will be eating outside, under the big tree," said Nate.

Everyone went outside, and Nate saved Silvia a seat beside him.

"You can sit here," offered Uncle Lupe, patting the seat beside him as he beckoned to Mama Joyce.

"No, thank you; I will sit on the other side of Nate," she declined.

Lupe said Grace, then they laughed and feasted late into the night.

Silvia helped the women clean up before retiring for the night. It had been a long day and being that she was still in the recovery stage, her energy was zapped.

"Knock, knock," said Nate, appearing in the doorway of Silvia's room.

"Checking on you one last time before I go to

bed—you need anything?"

"Nope, nothing at the moment. I like your friends."

"Yeah, they are good people. Well…see you in the morning, Silv."

"Ahh, my abuela was the only person that called me Silv. I like it," she said, smiling. "Wait…what does Nate stand for?"

"Nathaniel," he replied. "Yeah, Mom calls me Nathaniel when she is mad at me."

"OK, well goodnight, Natie!" she laughed.

"No, no … let's just stick with Nate. Natie, the gladiator, doesn't sound quite right! Get some sleep. I will see you in the morning," he repeated, closing the door behind him.

During the night, Silvia woke up with a desperate urge to go to the bathroom.

OMG, it's outside and it's pitch black out there…I gotta get Nate to go with me, she thought.

She slipped some shorts under her nightgown and ran across the hall.

The house was quiet; everyone was asleep.

She lightly tapped on the door…"Nate," she whisper-called.

No response.

She opened the door and stuck her head in. "Nate!" she tried again.

Still no response.

"Nate, wake up!" she hissed.

Still there was no response. She tiptoed into the

room and stood at his bedside.

"Nate...Nate, wake up, I have to use the bathroom."

Nate remained unresponsive and Silvia began to feel frustrated.

She leaned in and touched his arm, trying to wake him. Before she could blink, with one

swift move Nate grabbed her arm and flipped her into the bed. He quickly straddled her and had his hands around her throat!

"No, no, Papi," Silvia whimpered. She wiggled, kicked and whined beneath him, unable to break his grip.

"Nathaniel!" a shrill voice rang out from the hallway.

There stood Mama Joyce in the doorway with her hands on her hips. The sound of her voice awakened him and immediately brought him into reality.

Mama Joyce flipped on the lights.

"Boy, get off and let go of that girl before you kill her!"

He immediately released his grasp. "Silvia! My God, girl, don't ever sneak up on me like that, especially while I'm sleeping!" ordered Nate, scared now.

He then placed his face down in Silvia's chest, pausing for a moment to thank God that

he didn't kill her. Mama Joyce went back to her room.

"Really, what were you thinking? I mean, what

were you doing?" asked Nate as he got off her.

"Nothing. I woke up having to pee real bad. I tapped on the door, I even called you several times, but you didn't say anything," she explained. "I was only trying to wake you up. It's way too dark to go to the outhouse by myself!"

"OK, I understand, let's go. I'll take you now," he said, helping her up from the bed.

"Umm, I don't think that's going to be our issue anymore. You just made me pee in your bed!"

"Really, Silv? Come on!"

"Oh, noo Papi...don't blame me! You're the one who body-slammed and choked me! If it hadn't been for Mama Joyce, I would have been dead by now! Where is she, anyway?" Silvia said, looking towards the door.

"She must have gone back to her room. She probably heard you when you came to my door! Some things never change. I swear she has satellites for ears," said Nate, laughing. "Alright, come on, get up 'Pissy-Wissy'!" He extended his hand to help her up.

"You might wanna hit the shower though, before this equator heat makes you stink!

There's a closed in shower on the back porch."

"Ha, ha," said Silvia, rolling her eyes. "But now, where are you going to sleep? We don't have a couch."

"Probably with my momma," said Nate, still cracking jokes.

"Nooo, Nate, please don't tell your mom that I had an accident in your bed," Silvia pleaded.

"I'm just joking, I'm a soldier; I can camp out on the floor. But first, I have to clean this mattress and put it outside, so it can dry in the morning sun."

"Ay, ay..." Silvia began to speak in her native language.

Of course, Nate didn't understand a word!

Then, she reverted to English. "Noo...but Papi, everyone will know if you do that! I am truly sorry and embarrassed!"

"It's OK Pissy-Wissy," he chuckled.

"You clean the mattress while I go wash up. You can sleep with me for tonight, if you promise to be good," Silvia offered.

"Always a gentleman," replied Nate.

While she showered, Nate positioned his pillows to use as a divider between them, in her bed. After what she'd been through, he really wasn't sure about the idea and he really didn't want her to feel uncomfortable at any time. Besides, he knew that deep down a part of her was still scared. He was on his side and almost asleep when she slipped in beside him.

Apparently, she had gotten over her fear of the dark.

Keeping his promise, he stayed on his side and she stayed on hers. Shortly after daylight, Nate went back to his room, to get ready for the day. He and the fellows had work to do!

He met his mom in the kitchen, making breakfast.

"Morning, Mom."

71

"Hello, son," she answered sternly.

"Mom, what's wrong?"

"Nothing, you're grown."

"Mom, come on—what is it?"

"Are you sure that you know everything that you need to know about this woman? I can't believe that you would be sleeping with her! My goodness, and with me in the house—where is your respect?"

Nate threw his hands up in disgust. "First of all, Mom, you raised me better than that," protested Nate.

Then, he began to tell her everything. By the end of the story, she felt bad and saw Silvia in a whole new light. Actually, the information was more than she could handle. She had to pull out a chair and have a seat.

"Oh my, that poor girl. That explains her face, her body…poor child. Here I was, thinking that she had some kind of disease!" said Mama Joyce, still baffled.

"No, ma'am, Chris checked; she's fine."

"I'm glad, because I can see something happening: love is in the air."

"Mom, you have only seen us together for one day. How can you say that?"

"Son, I'm an old woman; besides, it only takes a few seconds to recognize love. I still think that you can do better, but something is definitely happening. You'd better get yourself under control, before you hurt her during the night. Please forgive me, son, for jumping to conclusions."

Suddenly, they heard the bedroom door opening and Silvia appeared.

"Good morning!" she said.

"Good morning," said Mama Joyce. "After that nightmare last night, did you get any sleep?"

Nate and Silvia's eyes met.

"Yes ma'am, I slept pretty well, I guess...certainly learned a lot about waking sleeping giants, though," she said, smiling then dropping her head.

"Don't feel bad, honey, I learned that lesson the hard way too. He'd just come home from a tour. I knew that he was tired, and I was trying to wake him up, to go to bed. Before I could even breathe, he had me! Bruno, my German Shepherd, started barking...that's what saved me."

"OK ladies, I am sitting right here," Nate reminded them. "Again, I apologize."

"Well they sure don't call him Gladiator for nothing," Silvia said sarcastically.

Both women looked at each other and burst out laughing. Nate, on the other hand, failed to see the humor.

"It's OK...we forgive you, son," said Mama Joyce, giving his face a little smack.

Seeing the need to change the subject, Nate said, "Man, it's been a long time since my momma made me breakfast."

"Yep, years," replied his mom.

"Silvia, I'm not sure what's on your agenda for today, but I ask that you stay close by. I will feel more secure once we beef up the security, but you're safe here. Get to know your new home and friends," advised Nate.

Over the ensuing months, Arkarma and Silvia became best friends. Every day she taught Silvia something about life in the Outback. Mama Joyce and Uncle Lupe became quite fond of each other as well. They took long evening strolls and he would take her fishing, in the fishing hole down the road. He even taught her how to can fruits and vegetables.

After the guys had improved security, they added a fully enclosed bathroom onto the back porch, including a tub, shower and toilet. For Nate, this meant no more late-night trips to the outhouse with the ladies and a daily hot shower himself. He was overjoyed that so far there was no sign of trouble.

Life was good on the Outback!

Arkarma had been teaching Silvia about different types of herbs and where to find them.

"Knock, knock," she said as she entered the cottage. "Hello, friend!"

"Hello friend, what's on the agenda for today?" replied Silvia.

"Today, we are going to find some herbs for your skin, and you can tell me what happened to it."

"I don't think that there is much that can be done for it. I've tried different creams," said Silvia, uncomfortably. "Nothing seems to work!"

"Those were man-made creams; we will make something from the good Lord's garden. It will work, wait and see. Now the only catch is, we will have to go into the town square and buy a few ingredients."

"Oh, I don't know about that," said Silvia. "I usually don't go anywhere without Nate."

"Girlie, you will be fine. Besides, I have my pistol right here." Arkarma pulled out her small pistol with a pink handle and handed it to Silvia. "Trust me, nobody wants to mess with a pregnant woman with a gun! I'll teach you how to use it, one day."

"Aww man, this is cute. Well, looks like we are ready," Silvia acquiesced.

"Yep, we should be back before the men get back."

The square was busy. People were everywhere! They came down from the Hills and neighboring towns to buy and sell their goods. Arkarma made sure to keep Silvia at her side always. After a few minutes of making their way through the crowd, Arkarma found the herbs that she was looking for.

She bought a lot of them. The man selling it was a short, fat, older white man.

Everything was fine until he began to speak.

At the sound of his voice, Silvia's heart dropped! She grew pale and began to shake; she'd never be able to forget that voice! It wasn't until he gave Arkarma back her change, that she panicked! How could she forget his short, thick, stubby fingers?

OMG, they are here!

The image of those ugly fingers was branded on her brain! She could recognize them anywhere! How could she ever forget those dirty fingernails? Immediately, she began to retreat, pulling Arkarma by the arm.

Not sure what was going on, Arkarma followed without haste.

Suddenly, Silvia turned her arm loose and took off in a mad sprint!

She ran all the way back to the farm.

As she entered the big gate, she began to scream Nate's name. "Nate, Nate!" She searched the house from room to room frantically.

There was no answer.

She ran out onto the back porch and found the bathroom door closed. She began to pound on it as if she could knock it down.

Nate's hot bath had put him to sleep.

His nap was over when he heard her screaming his name. Almost breaking his neck trying to get out of the tub, he quickly slipped into his drawers and opened the door.

"Silv, what's wrong?" he yelled. At the sight of his face, she passed out into his wet arms. Nate scooped her up and carried her to bed. He tried smacking her hand to make her regain consciousness.

Nothing.

Yelling her name wasn't working either. She was out! Akarma came flying into the room, yelling Silvia's name.

The sight of her passed out made Arkarma hysterical as well.

"Arkarma, I'm going to need you to calm down for me. I don't think that I can handle both of you right now. Tell me what happened," asked Nate.

Unfortunately, she had no answers and there was only one way to find out!

Arkarma reached for the glass of water on the dresser and threw its contents into Silvia's face. She woke up yelling Nate's name again.

"I'm right here," said Nate, holding her in his arms.

"They are here," gasped Silvia. "They found us and they're gonna get me!"

"What are you talking about?" Nate demanded.

She confessed to the outing and tried to explain what she saw, while fighting back her tears. Overwhelmed with emotion, Silvia began to sob and hyperventilate.

"You're home now; it's okay, breathe...Are you sure it was him? I thought he always had on his mask," asked Nate.

"Yes, he was the one who wanted the party the most!

I could never forget his short, nasty fingers. He visited almost every day!"

"OK, I will go check it out."

"Nate, noo…don't leave me!"

"Come on, babe…" pleaded Nate. He needed to see for himself.

"NO," she said firmly.

"Alright, I won't go; try to rest, I will check it out

tomorrow. Arkarma and I will be outside."

"I'm sorry, Gladiator," Arkarma said ruefully. "I should have never taken her off the property.

It's just that she has been feeling so bad about the way she looks. I was only trying to help by making an herbal cream. It seems like I have created another problem. My husband is going to kill me."

"No, don't worry. She will be fine. It will just take some time," Nate assured her.

"I feel terrible! I guess I will just go home and whip up this sauze," said Arkarma.

CHAPTER FIVE

Nate had Mama Joyce looking after Silvia while she slept.

He, on the other hand, couldn't rest until he checked out the guy selling herbs in the square. There is no way that they could have found us. I was careful, and we are thousands of miles away; partly by ocean, thought Nate, as he searched the square.

Finally, he found his stand. Yes, he did have short, cruddy fingers like Old J; but the man looked nothing like him! This guy only had three teeth in his whole mouth! How could she have possibly missed that? Nate was relieved and could not wait to tell Silvia the good news! Back at the house, he found Silvia and Mama Joyce sitting at the kitchen table having coffee. His mom was also relieved to hear the news, although there was a part of her that was still skeptical.

After only a few weeks of using Arkarma's sauze, there was a noticeable improvement in Silvia's skin.

"I can't believe how well your sauze is working!" Silvia enthused.

"I told you it would, you look like a totally different person," Arkarma agreed.

"I know, right?" The burn marks are beginning to lighten up and they're shrinking. The craters are still there, but I don't mind. I almost feel like a woman again," said Silvia.

"Oh, girl, stop it! With those curves, you are definitely a woman. A woman who has captured the eye and heart of a certain gentleman; he can't stop looking at you!"

"No, he doesn't see me like that."

"What, Silvia? Please. You know that you like him too," laughed Arkarma.

"Anyway...what was it that you wanted to do today?" asked Silvia, trying to avoid answering.

"I thought we might gather some berries. Dhunganda and I would love to have you guys over tonight for a bonfire under the stars. Sounds romantic, huh?" said Arkarma, smiling.

"Yes, sounds like fun. I will ask Nate about it, when he comes home. He's been working hard, trying to help Uncle Lupe add on to his home," said Silvia.

It seemed as if Nate had love on his mind as well. While working, he realized that his feelings for Silvia were growing. He'd been so busy, hardly spending any quality time with her. It was noonday, which meant quitting time. It was too hot to be roofing,

so he decided to ask her out. He came home to find two beautiful ladies sitting under the tree, drinking lemonade and peeling apples.

"Hi Silv, you wanna go on a fishing trip with me later on?" Nate yelled across the yard.

"You mean like a date?" Mama Joyce yelled back.

Nate sternly gave her the "Momma, please, I got this" look.

"Yeah, sure—but you're touching the fish...and the worms!" Silvia replied.

"OK then, it's a date," said Nate, winking at his momma.

"Be ready at 4 o'clock."

"I will...but first I'm going to pick berries with Arkarma."

"Remember to be careful," said Nate.

"Yes, I know. Never get too comfortable, always observe my surroundings and stay alert: there is always something out here that would like to eat you! You see, I'm learning," she said, gesturing for him to go on into the cottage.

Nate laughed.

"Wow, aren't you becoming the little Outbacker," Mama Joyce chimed in.

Silvia ignored her comment and said, "Be right back, going to Arkarma's," then she

made a dash to her neighbor's cottage. Obviously, running was something that she and Nate had in common. Arkarma saw her as she came speeding through the yard. Thinking that something was wrong, she met her at the door.

"What's the matter?" she asked.

"Nothing. I got a date," Silvia told her, smiling.

"With Gladiator?"

"Yes, who else? We're supposed to be going on a

81

fishing trip at 4 p.m. I thought it would be nice to put a girl's touch on it. I want to make it a picnic."

"That would be nice," said Arkarma.

"Only, I don't have a picnic basket and Mama Joyce has warned me to stay out of her kitchen," Silvia said. "Can you help me?"

"Of course I can, a picnic doesn't require a lot of cooking," said Arkarma. "First thing, how about you go ask Uncle Lupe for a jar of his blackberry wine, while I see what I can throw together real quick. Take Dhunganda's bike."

As suggested, Silvia left headed for the rear of the property, trying to locate Uncle Lupe. She thought it was amazing how they all lived on the same land, yet had enough distance between them for privacy.

Uncle Lupe was outside digging a flowerbed in front of his porch.

Hearing the news about the date excited him too. He retrieved one of the oldest wines he had in the pantry. Then he continued to work on his garden. It seemed as if Lupe had a few tricks up his sleeve, himself. The flowerbed was for Mama Joyce. He said that he wanted to surprise her with a truck full of flowers when he picked her up.

"How sweet! Looks like the old folks would be spending the evening in the dirt," Silvia laughed. "Well, thanks for the wine, Unc. Unfortunately, I must run, I'm a little pressed for time."

"Yes, yes, go...you kids enjoy!"

By the time Silvia made it back to Arkarma's she

was feeling a little fatigued.

Once again, her bestie came through.

The picnic basket was sitting on the counter, waiting for her.

"Look at what I found...some shaved brisket from last night's dinner, mild goat cheese and crackers, cubed papaya and a few of the fresh berries we picked earlier."

"It's perfect! Now, there's only one problem; how can I get it past Mama Joyce?"

"Leave it here, tell Gladiator that you forgot something!"

"Yes! You know what? Never in a million years could I have found a better friend. You

have been so good to me, Arkarma," said Silvia gratefully.

"Ha, we are all that we've got! Besides, my family lives in the Hills. I barely talk to

anyone in these parts," said Arkarma. "Now, enough of the mushy stuff—go get ready!"

Time flew by! Before she knew it, Nate was knocking on her bedroom door.

He was amazed at how good she looked in jeans and a tank top.

"You ready?" asked Nate.

"¡Si Papi, vamonos!" she replied.

"Excuse me?"

"I said, yes daddy, let's go!"

Nate blushed.

"Can I drive?" Silvia asked.

"What?" asked Nate.

"I wanna drive," said Silvia.

"Can you drive, and can you drive a Hummer, are the questions," laughed Nate.

"Yes, I can drive. My dad owned three Hummers, I'll have you know!"

With no other objection, Nate his threw his hands up in the air.

"Alright, but I will have to start it for you."

Silvia went to pick up the basket from Arkarma, then they were on their way.

Within a few minutes, Nate realized letting her drive might have been a mistake!

She drove like a mad woman! She surely had Hummer experience!

He could only smile as he watched the wild woman in her emerge as she drove.

She was a real-life Daisy Duke!

Nate gave directions as she drove. It looked like they were in the middle of nowhere!

"Are you sure that you know where you're going?" asked Silvia.

"Yes, I'm sure—actually, we are here. We have to go the rest of the way

on foot. Park here," he suggested.

They hiked through the woods for about 10 minutes and Silvia talked all the

way. Suddenly, Nate stopped and so did she.

"What's wrong?" she asked.

"Nothing, listen…"

"Is that running water?"

Nate pointed upward towards the hills, and Silvia ran towards the sound.

The sight of the cascading waterfall took her breath away! Nate helped her down the hill to the opening. While she set up the picnic, Nate surprised her with a song on his harmonica. She danced as he played.

The picnic went well. Nate totally forgot about fishing.

Instead, he enjoyed their quality time. He enjoyed talking, laughing and learning more about this mystery woman, whom he was falling in love with. Before they knew it, it was time to go home. Again, Nate watched Silvia as she drove, wondering what he was getting himself into. Whatever it was, he couldn't stop it.

"Can I get you to pull over a second?" asked Nate.

She pulled to the side of the road.

"There is one more thing that I want to show you," he said.

"Why are we just sitting here?"

"Wait a minute, you will see."

A few minutes later, a beautiful cast of the setting sun came across the sky.

"Wow, look at that sunset," Silvia said reverently. "I have seen sunsets before, but none as beautiful as this one. It's absolutely amazing! "Oooh, and look, Nate, 'roos! A mom and five little joeys went hopping towards the sunset. I have never seen them this close before!"

"Beautiful creatures, aren't they? They are considered sacred in these parts. Especially to the Aborigine. OK ma'am, we must go. This area is beautiful, but it's getting dark and we are very close to the watering hole."

"Say no more," said Silvia.

Nate started the Hummer and they were off. Daisy Duke was on the road again, not one pothole being missed. Nate could only smile, as he held on to the overhead support handle for dear life! It was so amazing that only a few months ago, she was

fighting for her life. While he was caught up in his thoughts, Silvia reached over and put her hand on Nate's knee.

"Calmese, calmese," (calm down, calm down) she said.

"Both hands on the wheel, woman," Nate demanded, pointing at the steering wheel.

"Come on, you've always had my life in your hands. Now, the one time that I have yours in mine, you're all nervous?" laughed Silvia.

"Yeah well, I just want to make it home in one piece. I would like to check on Mama Joyce."

"Well, I got a feeling that Mama Joyce is doing just fine. Haven't you noticed that a certain someone has been occupying her time?"

"Yes, I noticed that she has been spending a lot of time with Uncle Lupe."

"From what I hear, she is adding a woman's

touch to his cottage. Today, he dug her a flowerbed. Monday, they will be painting the outside. If I didn't know better, I'd say old Lupe is smitten," said Silvia.

"Oh yeah, then I need to get over there," said Nate. "Helping Dhunganda work in the hills is making me miss out on a few things."

"Nate, no...don't go over there messing with them! She has raised you to be a wonderful man. It's her turn now, so let her live...have a little fun."

"I guess so, Silv ... I guess you are right," said Nate, sighing and thinking. "My mom has a boyfriend..."

"A man," Silvia chimed in, smiling. "Everybody needs somebody. At least you know where to find her."

"Yeah, old Lupe is a stand-up kind of guy. She's in good hands. By the way, when did you get so experienced in love?"

"Probably when I first felt loved," she laughed, raising her eyebrows.

"Hmmm," said Nate, smiling. "Yeah, well, I guess I have my own issues to worry about, like getting you a gun."

"Yes, I want one like Arkarma's; it's small and I can handle it!"

"Really? How do you know that, may I ask?" queried Nate, as Silvia pulled up into their driveway.

"Well, since the incident in the square, Arkarma and I have been doing a lil girlie target practice. I will have you know, not only can I shoot a pistol, but my bow and arrow skills are improving as well. Soon, I'm going to be a pretty good markswoman," Silvia announced proudly.

"I see, so what else has Arkarma been teaching you?" questioned Nate, turning in his seat. I thought you were making pottery, or canning; you know—domestic things."

"We are. It's all a part of the plan. When I get myself together, we want to open a stand in the square. Latino and Aborigine style!" She told him excitedly. "And now that you see that I can handle the Hummer, I want to go to Manchester, a few minutes away. Akarma said there is a market there, where I can find a lot of my native foods. I want to make some for you."

"You cook?" asked Nate.

"Yes, I can cook! I may come from a family that spoiled me, but my abuela made sure that I learned. She said that no man wants a woman that doesn't know her way around the kitchen."

"Really! I haven't seen you boil water since we have been here."

"That's because your mama won't let me!" exclaimed Silvia, laughing.

"True, true," laughed Nate, agreeing.

"Well, it really seems that you and Arkarma have everything planned out. You're cooking, shopping, shooting…I guess there is no reason for me not to give you this."

Reaching underneath his seat, Nate pulled out a medium-sized box, opened it and handed it to her.

"No, no, Nate! No!" said Silvia as she bounced in

her seat like a kid with a new toy. "That's the one! Thank you, thank you!" Then she leaned in and planted a peck on his lips, their first kiss.

"Hey, you know that was supposed to be my move, right?"

"You snooze, you lose, Papi!"

"Papi ... that means 'daddy', right?" asked Nate, reconfirming.

"Yes, it does," replied Silvia, smiling.

They both laughed and decided not to extend the conversation any further.

Silvia couldn't believe that she was holding her own gun, with "Silv" engraved on it. "Come on, let's go try it out!" She jumped out of the truck and met him on the passenger's side. Then, she placed the gun on the hood of the Hummer and threw her arms around Nate's neck.

"You just don't know how I thank God for you and my new life. I am so happy!" She gushed, laying her head on his chest and inhaling his scent, as she fought back tears. "OK now, let's go. Let me show you what this thing can do, Nate!"

With the gun in one hand and Nate's hand in the other, Silvia dragged him around the house like she might a child.

Nate set out old milk jugs on top of the privacy fence. "OK miss lady, let me see what Arkarma has taught you."

To his amazement, she wasn't too bad. However, she still needed proper training. He needed to know that she could use the gun with safety and control.

"Look, stand like this. Spread your legs a little, so that you can maintain your balance when she kicks." As he stood close behind her with his hand around her waist, his eyes couldn't help but be drawn to her curves. It was in that moment, as he held her that he was sure: as far as he was concerned, no other man would ever touch her again!

"Now remember, baby, it's a tool, not a toy!" Baby! Thought Nate. Baby? Man, did I just say that? Nate was amazed himself at how smoothly that rolled off his tongue.

Silvia heard him too. He could tell, although she pretended not to.

They shot off a couple more rounds, then retired for the night.

The next morning, Nate awakened to a strange noise—silence.

No banging pots, pans or bacon frying...nothing but silence.

The clock said eight o'clock and Mama Joyce could never have slept past six. What's going on? Where is she, he wondered?

Oh, I know she didn't, he thought, tumbling to an uncomfortable suspicion. He ran out of his bedroom and hurried down the hall to her room.

"Knock, knock," he said. He waited, but there was no answer.

"Mama, are you alright?" he called again. Still there was no answer.

Nate opened her door to find a nice, clean, quiet room with a bed that was still made up. He slammed the door, stormed down the hall to Silvia's room, and barged right in.

"You are not going to believe this," he yelled, scaring her awake.

She immediately went into panic mode, jumping to her feet in the bed and wrapping her bed covers around her. Instantly, he realized what he had done and ran to comfort her.

"Calm down, it's me…I'm sorry, I didn't mean to scare you. It's just, mama didn't come home last night."

"Really, Nate? You almost scared the life out of me, just to say that? Chill out! Your mom is a grown woman, and it's not like you don't know where she is!"

"I don't care, she's still my mama!" he roared. "If I don't stay out all night, then she can't stay out all night, either! Trust and believe, we are gonna talk about this!"

A knock at the front door saved her from having to hear any more. She gratefully slid back down into her bed and pulled the covers over her head. Nate went to the door, still upset. He figured it was Mama Joyce, but it was Dhunganda instead. Nate said nothing, just opened the door and walked away, letting him in.

"What's wrong with you?" Dhunganda asked.

Nothing, but Mama Joyce didn't come home last night! Guess she stayed at Uncle Lupe's all night!"

"Ummm, are you sure about that? I just talked to her a minute ago. She's on the side of the house, over there under the big tree, peeling taters. Says she's making tater cakes for your breakfast."

Nate ran out onto the wrap around porch to see for himself!

Sure enough, there she was, sitting there with a big jar of orange juice; peeling away! He turned and went back inside.

"Man, I feel like an idiot!" Nate admitted.

"Come on bro, mom has found love again," Dhunganda said. "You should be happy for her...and it's with a good guy we all know and love."

"Yeah, I guess I'm not used to sharing her. I'll get over it," Nate resolved.

"Well, I think that you need a break. Let's ride into Georgetown and hang out; like a bro-day or something."

"I can't leave Silvia," Nate responded.

"See, that is what I'm talking about. You should be glad Uncle Lupe is seeing after your mom, seems like you have your hands full here, with your own li'l filly."

"Yeah, you are right. But you have to understand, she has been through a lot. If we could only get her over the nightmares…" reflected Nate.

"I understand; tell you what, I will be back to pick you up. I will bring Arkarma with me, she will keep Silvia occupied. Those two always find something to do. As a matter of fact, I think she taught Arkarma how to crochet. Now, she's been talking about teaching me to crochet baby booties."

"Ahh, I see—so this little bro-day isn't really about me clearing my head. Instead, it's about you getting away from your pregnant wife," laughed Nate.

"Pregnant and hormonal wife," added Dhunganda. "No, seriously, we will be back in plenty of time for me to make baby booties with her."

"OK. Bro-day!" laughed Nate.

The bro-day went well. The guys really enjoyed hanging out and they were back just before dark. Not able to resist it anymore, Nate decided to pay Uncle Lupe a visit.

He found him outside watering Mama Joyce's flowers, while the smell of pot roast floated from his kitchen window.

"What's up, old friend?" Nate greeted him.

"Nothing much, Gladiator. Where have you been hiding out, and what can I do for you?"

"Well, seems like you have something that belongs to me," said Nate with a fake laugh.

"Oh yeah, what?" asked Uncle Lupe sarcastically. "You know, I've been waiting on you to show up."

He turned off the water, threw the hose down and wiped his hands on his old overalls.

"Walk with me, son."

He and Nate walked toward the old shed in the back of the yard.

"Well, Gladiator, it's like this…I have never been one with a whole lot of words, so look…I have been spending a lot of time with your mom, and honestly, I have become quite fond of her. This is it," said Lupe as he reached into his pocket, pulling out a ring box and opening it.

"I wanna marry your Mama. That is, if it is okay with you."

Nate stood there speechless, gazing at the ring.

"Gladiator, Gladiator! Say something, boy!" exclaimed Uncle Lupe.

"Oh, yeah...yes, you can marry her, I just wasn't expecting you to say that! Actually, the situation with her is only one of the reasons that I came over. I also wanted to talk to you about this."

Nate reached into his pocket and pulled out a ring box as well. Inside was a red ruby engagement ring.

"What...really? Is this for the Misses?"

"Yes," said Nate. "I came over to talk about mom, but I also wanted to know what you

thought about it."

"You wanna know what I think?" asked Lupe.

Without saying another word, he threw his old hat off his head and began to do one of his native dances.

"What does that mean?"

"It means, go get her, boy! This is the Aborigine marriage dance! Well, don't just stand there, go get your woman! No, I tell you what; just get out of the way." Lupe pushed him aside. "You're stopping me from getting to mine!" with that, Uncle Lupe marched back towards the cottage.

They laughed together and both headed out to get their girls. Mama Joyce was already there, as usual.

She was inside washing the blackberries they had picked earlier.

"I think I will make some blackberry cobbler for dessert," said Mama Joyce.

"Sounds good to me. Boy, am I glad that I caught you before you got your hands all messed up in flour," said Lupe.

"What do you mean?"

"I mean this," he said, grabbing her blackberry juice-stained hands and leading her into the middle of the floor.

"Joyce, you're a beautiful woman and I have enjoyed every moment that you have spent here. So, what I am trying to say is, 'why leave'?"

Then, he dropped to one knee and pulled out the ring box.

"Oh my!" yelled Mama Joyce. She threw her free hand over her eyes and blackberry juice was smeared across her face.

"Will you marry me?" asked Lupe.

Mama Joyce stood speechless, with tears rolling down her face.

"Aye...darling, can you decide soon? I'm an old man and these old knees can't take much longer," he pleaded.

She finally answered.

"Yes, yes old man, I will marry you! Now, come on, get up!" She assisted him back to his feet.

Lupe placed the ring on her finger and gave her a kiss.

I gotta go…I gotta go show Nate," said Mama Joyce, tears of joy still flowing.

"No need," came a voice from behind her.

Nate was standing in the doorway, having watched the whole thing!

"Nate, Nathaniel…" she cried, running to her son with her arms open wide. "Look, I'm getting married!"

"Yes, mom, I know; you have my blessing…congratulations!"

Relieved, she began to jump up and down, clapping her hands.

As for Lupe, well, he did a few more steps of the marriage dance.

"OK, Gladiator…Go! It's your turn," said Uncle Lupe, giving him a thumbs up.

Forgetting all about the Hummer, Nate took off in a sprint. He went down the driveway, one-fourth of a mile to their side of the property. He was going to claim his bride!

He reached the cottage in no time! As soon as he stepped onto the porch, he began to call her name.

"Silvia! Silvia! Silv, where are you?"

He ran through the house, searching for her. There was no answer from her, but the sound of gunshots stopped him in his tracks! "Man, she's practicing again!

This girl and her gun!" he said to himself.

As he exited the back porch, he understood why she didn't hear him calling; she had some ear plugs.

"Silvia!" he called out once again, but she couldn't

hear him. He stood there for a moment, contemplating how he could get her attention without getting shot. Walking up to her was not an option! She was an untrained rookie with a new gun! The mere thought of it made him nervous. Moving off instinct, Nate picked up a big rock and threw it into her goldfish pond.

The large splash caught her eye.

When she dropped her gun hand to her side for a closer look, Nate quickly tackled her from behind. He dropped her so hard, the gun went flying in the other direction. Silvia began to scream for dear life! Of course, she thought that the cartel had found her. Nate quickly rolled her over, kicking and screaming, while still straddling her.

"Silvia, Silvia, babe...it's me, Nate!"

"Why? What, what is wrong with you, Papi?" she shouted.

Nate took her ear plugs out and said, "Can you please stop yelling?"

"Stop yelling? You tackled me!" she said, indignantly.

Then she did one of the things he loved about her most; she started rattling off in her native tongue. He didn't understand a word she said, but he knew it wasn't good!

Noticing her aggravation, Nate decided he'd better hurry up with the question.

"Silv, I have something to ask you."

"OK, but can we get up first?"

"No, nope...I think this is the perfect position. I

have you right where I want you—covered." He leaned in and braced his hands on the ground beside her head.

"OK, what is it?" she asked, resigned.

"Silv, I have fallen in love with you. I don't ever want another man to look at or touch you again! Plus, I have found—"

Silvia quickly interrupted.

"Sorry Papi, but can you hurry...I'm on a rock...!"

"Really? I bet it's not as pretty as this one," said Nate, taking the ring box out of his shirt pocket and exposing the big red ruby!

She was speechless! Suddenly, the rock and the ache in her back weren't that important anymore. As a matter of fact, they disappeared!

"Marry me, Silvia," said Nate.

She relaxed in the dirt, rock and all, tears rolling down her cheeks.

Then, she closed her eyes and began to speak in Spanish again.

"I'm not sure, honey, but was that a yes? Did you say yes?" asked Nate, desperately.

"Si—yes, yes Papi, I will marry you!" cried Silvia.

Nate stood and pulled her up into his arms, placed the ring on her finger, then turned her around for a kiss.

"Oh, guess what," said Nate. "Mama and Lupe are getting married too!"

"What? How do you feel about it?"

"I'm good, it's fine. Besides, I have my own woman to see about," said Nate.

"You sure do," replied Silvia, getting on her tiptoes for another kiss.

With one swift move, Nate scooped her up and threw her over his shoulder to carry her in the house.

"Noo, Papi, wait...my gun!" Silvia yelled.

"Man, this woman and her gun!" thought Nate. He said to her, "I will be out here to get it first thing in the morning, babe!"

"Ha, what about using the flashlight?"

Nate ignored her and kept walking. "You know, Nate, I think the flashlight is in my room," said Silvia Again, he quietly walked.

"OK love, first thing in the morning will be fine."

Having had enough excitement for one day, they both retired for the night.

Love was in the air! The new engagements were the talk of the town!

Silvia couldn't wait to ask Arkarma to be her matron of honor.

The weddings brought Silvia and Mama Joyce closer than ever. Nate loved it; they were finally a family. The women decided to have a double wedding. The date was set for September 13th and the next three months were chaos!

The women ordered Uncle Lupe to build a gazebo for the ceremony. Silvia had Nate repaint the cottage in more vibrant hues, to incorporate more of her Latino flair. Meanwhile, both women kept adding finishing touches to their weddings.

Nate finally turned Silvia loose with the Hummer.

She, Mama Joyce, Arkarma and a few more bridesmaids kept the roads hot shopping, shopping, shopping! They didn't mind the fact that the Hummer didn't have a back seat. It had AC and was a definite upgrade from the old jalopy.

They decided to keep it simple, with a little Latino-Aborigine infusion.

"Mama Joyce, I noticed Nate hasn't asked anyone to be his best man yet," said Silvia while shopping.

"I know, what is he waiting for?" Arkarma replied.

"I don't know, I think he is wishing that Lou could be here."

"Yes, I know," said Mama Joyce, "but in the meantime, the show must go on."

"You're right," Silvia replied.

Everyone was pitching in for the reception. Uncle Lupe's cousins were roasting two hogs. Arkarma and her sisters were decorating and the friends from the Hills were bringing homemade booze. Silvia saw the opportunity to show Mama Joyce her cooking skills and took advantage of it, choosing to make several Hispanic dishes.

Things seemed to be coming together nicely; that is, except for the male attire.

Uncle Lupe was refusing to wear anything except a pair of overalls or his native

loin cloth and beads. Exhausted from going back and forth with him, they decided to put Nate in charge of the male attire.

Two days before the wedding, Nate came home to find the girls in session. They were sitting around the kitchen table and makeup was everywhere!

"How do I look?" asked Silvia.

Nate almost didn't recognize her. "Beautiful," he replied, "but can I talk to you for a second?"

They stepped into the hallway. "Look, babe. I think you look beautiful. I want you to feel comfortable on your big day. What I want you to know is that I think that you are just as beautiful, every day. Only you and I truly know how far you have come. Your skin is beautiful, you may never get rid of all the craters. You see them as craters—I see them as battle scars. A battle that you survived and won.

"So basically, the one thing I want you to know is, that I would proudly carry you on my arm as my Queen, any day—made up, or not!"

Tears began to fill Silvia's eyes. She threw her arms around Nate's neck and gave him a kiss that left him a little dizzy.

"Thanks, my love," she whispered. She quickly went into the bathroom, washed it all off and returned to the ladies at the table.

"Let's try it again, but lighter," she suggested.

Nate was still standing in the hallway reminiscing about their kiss.

"Man, I gotta remember to compliment her often," he thought as he left them to their girlie fun.

The big day, September 13th, had finally arrived. The entire property was buzzing. People were running, working and preparing in every direction.

Arkarma's sisters were busy decorating the gazebo in Uncle Lupe's front lawn.

Uncle Lupe's cousins were out back preparing their freshly roasted hogs. The rest of the women were in Uncle Lupe's kitchen, getting the food ready for the reception.

Meanwhile, the wedding parties had been separated. The women were at Arkarma's and the men were at Nate's cottage.

"I can't wait for the ladies to see what I have put together. I know they think we are really gonna look 'jacked up'," said Nate.

They were all laughing, enjoying joke after joke, when there was a knock at the door.

Dhungana answered it.

"Ahh, hello; is my boy Nate here?"

Recognizing the voice, Nate literally ran out of his room. He was speechless.

"What...how? Lou, man, who told you? How did you find me? How did you get here?" The questions went on and on.

"Ha...is this a wedding, or an interrogation?" asked Lou, laughing.

The old friends hugged. Then, Nate introduced him to everyone.

"Well, no time to waste...come on, we have your outfit hanging in Silvia's closet," Uncle Lupe directed.

"We had to hide it from Nate," said Dhunganda.

"Wait, am I in the wedding? What could you

possibly need me to do?" said Lou sarcastically, while looking at Nate."

"You could be my best man."

"Well guess what, Bubba, I already am," laughed Lou. "Yeah, yeah I heard how you were down here moping around, wishing I were here!"

"Now, how in the world did you manage to hear that? You weren't even supposed to know my location," said Nate, laughing too.

"Man, I work for the government. I've learned a few tricks...Gladiator," said Lou.

"Oh no, you are going to tell me who your informant is…there's a freaking mole in the family!"

They all laughed and continued to get dressed.

"Let's hustle guys, our ride will be here soon," said Uncle Lupe.

"Calm down, old man. We're gonna get you to your lady," said one of the groomsmen.

Again, they laughed.

Things were not going as smoothly for the ladies. Arkarma had gained weight due to the pregnancy and her dress was a little too tight. The lady that practiced doing their makeup was sick, forcing the girls to wing it for themselves. Arkarma's cousin left her shoes at home in the Hills; the house was total chaos!

Meanwhile, Silvia was fighting to keep her bridezilla under control! This could not be happening—they were pressed for time, the wedding was in a few minutes and everyone was still trying to get dressed!

"What am I going to do about my shoes?" wailed Arkarma's cousin.

"Don't wear any," suggested the wedding planner. "As a matter of fact, nobody wears any shoes—not even you, Silvia! It's hot, the dresses aren't that long. We live in the outback! I think it would be cute."

"No shoes it is…OK, nobody wears shoes, but please polish your toes!" announced Silvia.

"We will just return the shoes for the money, sweetheart," chimed in Mama Joyce, trying to be supportive.

Mama Joyce was the first one dressed.

"Silvia, can I help you get dressed, if you don't mind? You will be my only daughter-in-law, and I won't get this chance again."

"Please do, Mama Joyce, I would be honored for you to help me. As of today, you are my mother," said Silvia.

"Well, with that said, I have your something borrowed, something blue…these are the pearls I bought right before I retired. This is the blue sapphire ring Nate's dad bought me one summer on vacation…will you wear them?"

"With honor," said Silvia graciously.

The two hugged and shed a few tears.

"Well, I guess the first thing we should do for each other, is not mess up our makeup," Silvia smiled.

"I agree," said Mama Joyce. "Now, let me help you into your dress."

CHAPTER SIX

Silvia's dress was off the shoulders and form-fitting, showing curves but not too tight. She chose to wear her hair in an updo, with a ring of flowers in it.

Mama Joyce's dress was a cream lace, mid-length A line dress. She too, wore an updo with a single flower in her hair. The bridesmaids' dresses were canary yellow, and they carried fresh flowers from Arkarma's wildflower garden.

Suddenly, a loud noise like the sound of rolling wheels pulled up outside.

"Our ride is here!" yelled Arkarma.

They stepped outside to find a wagon with several bales of hay on it.

"Come on ladies, we are going to a wedding...hayride style!" called the driver as he helped everyone aboard.

"I wonder what our men are wearing," mused Silvia as the wagon rocked and reeled slowly, trying to get the ladies to their destination. "I don't know; hopefully anything besides loin cloths and beads," said Mama Joyce, cringing. All the ladies laughed. The laughter had just ended when they pulled up to Lupe's property at the same time as the men did.

"Oh my," said Mama Joyce. She almost couldn't believe her eyes!

Sitting in the other wagon on bales of hay, were seven handsome men! They were sporting black overalls, white button-down shirts and canary yellow bow ties!

"Oooh, I think I wanna kiss my man now," said Silvia, thinking out loud.

"Hold your horses, missy, he's not quite yours just yet," replied Mama Joyce.

On cue, the music began to play, and each man walked his woman down the aisle;

starting with Arkarma and Dhunganda and ending with Nate and Silvia.

"You look amazing," he whispered into her ear, and gave her a small peck on the neck.

"Thank you, and your mama said no kissing. Not yet, anyway!" she replied.

"Pssh! When have I ever listened to my mom; but, OK... I will wait, because in a few minutes you will be Mrs. Nathaniel Brodgen!"

"'Mrs. Gladiator', I can't wait," said Silvia rapturously.

Nate smiled, he knew that he'd found his rib.

The ceremony was beautiful. The most touching part was when Mama Joyce and Uncle Lupe kissed. You never get too old for love.

When it came time for Silvia and Nate's nuptials,

Nate hesitated.

Silvia wondered what was going on.

Then, he began...

"I went on a mission, for a friend; or at least I thought that I was.

It turned out that the mission was for me. It was rough, but it led me to you.

That's why before I place the band on your finger, I'd like to give you another

ring. It's a black pearl. Black pearls are very valuable because they reside in the uttermost deepest parts of the ocean.

Silvia, this pearl represents you. Only you and I know what we have been through,

and I must tell you, you were worth the dive."

Tears began to lap under Silvia's chin. Forget the makeup, it was gone!

Her hand was trembling so bad, Nate had to hold it in order to put the ring on her finger.

The pastor continued and then Silvia placed the wedding band on his finger.

By the time they were finished, she felt as if she was walking on air! Never in her wildest dreams had she ever thought that she could feel this way...complete.

Shortly after the toast and first dances, Nate was interrupted by a tap on the shoulder.

"Lou, man, what's up?"

"Well my friend, it's sad to say, but I can't stay. I'm supposed to be on a stakeout, but the truth is I'm here in the Outback sharing one of the biggest days of my friend's life. Now, I must get going."

"I understand, but first I must know if you've heard anything from the cartel or the compound? Silvia thinks that she saw one of them in the square. She's paranoid and has nightmares."

"It wasn't him," mumbled Lou.

"How can you be so sure?" asked Nate.

"Because I too…complete my missions. Trust me, she will never see those enemies again!"

"What did you do?"

"I completed the job. I had a special GPS installed on the Hummer. When I saw that you were out of harm's way, I finished it."

"You blew it up?"

"Smithereens!" confirmed Lou. "I knew that you wouldn't be able to live without looking over your shoulder. I

also knew that you didn't have the heart to do it. To tell you the truth, I am kind of getting tired of it myself. This kind of life is becoming draining…stressful. I'm at the point where I'm looking for some peace. I just want to live, like you."

"Well, I can tell you, you never truly begin to live until you give your life to Christ.

I've been asking you for a while; are you ready now?"

"No, man, there are still some things that I need to work on; get right ... you know what I mean?"

"No, Lou, I don't. Let's step over here out of the

crowd for a minute, so we can talk." Nate gestured to the side of the room.

"This is what so many people don't understand God says 'come as you are', and he means just that! He means crying, broken, smoking, stripping, cussing, whatever it is, because he is merciful and just enough to meet you, right where you are. Those things that you think that you need to fix could take you five, ten, maybe twenty years...that's if you're even able to fix them at all. What could take you a lifetime to fix, God has the power to deliver you from in seconds.

"Think about it, if we were able to fix ourselves...save ourselves, there would be no reason for Jesus. It would mean that he died," explained Nate. "Man, all it takes is one conscious decision, to accept him as Lord and Savior; all of your slate is wiped clean. Sin and debts, forgiven..."

Lou stood there speechless, just taking it all in.

"OK, I'm ready," said Lou.

"Seriously?" asked Nate.

"Yes, seriously. Just tell me what I need to do."

Nate led him through the sinners' prayer. In the corner, in the middle of a wedding reception, Lou gave his life to Christ! Nate was so overwhelmed, he was in tears.

"Man, when I tell you that this has been the best day of my life, believe me!

Not only did I gain a bride; I gained a brother as well. Now, make sure you find a Bible-based church to go to; take your wife and babies to church," advised

Nate, hugging Lou tightly.

"I will, my brother...I love you. I have a few more farewells and then I must go. Live in peace my friend, you and the wifey. I'm going to say goodbye for now, but you will see me again..." said Lou as he walked away.

"Wait, so you have known my location all this time?" asked Nate.

"Who do I work for?" asked Lou, wryly.

"Yeah, OK, OK." Once again the old friends separated.

On his way out of the yard, Lou approached Mama Joyce.

"Walk with me, please," he whispered.

She accompanied him to the big gate at the end of the driveway.

"Well, Mama, again it's time to depart for now; but first I have a little something for you."

He handed her a harmonica. She opened it up and looked at the keyboard.

"It's just like the other one, right?" she asked.

"Yes, ma'am, and it's only in case of emergency or if you really need me. Remember, wait for me to answer, then destroy it! Oh, and Nate still doesn't know that you are my informant. Let's keep it that way! Hopefully, the next time I hear from you I will be an uncle."

Hugging him tightly, Mama Joyce said, "Goodbye, son."

"Never goodbye, but see you later," replied Lou.

He signaled for his driver and departed.

On the way back, Uncle Lupe met her halfway. They walked back down the driveway holding hands like teenagers in love. Of course, she excused herself long enough to hide her secret phone; then it was back to the party!

Silvia was struggling to teach Nate how to cha cha the Latino way.

"Ay, ay Papi … I do not understand how a man can run so fast with two left feet!"

"I don't think that I am quite ready for this," confessed Nate.

"Neither are my feet," laughed Silvia.

Their last dance of the night was to a soft and slow song. Silvia got on her tiptoes and whispered a question into Nate's ear.

"Babe, what will we tell our children?"

He whispered back, "The truth!"

Nate and Silvia quietly slipped away while family and friends danced into the wee hours of the night. Both anxious and nervous about consummating the marriage, they rode home, holding hands in silence. As Nate fidgeted with the lock on the front door, Silvia broke the silence.

"So, question...what now, soldier? You finished the mission, you got the girl; what's next?"

"Now that the mission is accomplished, I carry her into the Happily Ever After," he replied, smiling. Then he swooped her up into his arms and carried her across the threshold.

It was honeymoon night!

Nate was very nervous about consummating their marriage. He knew the ordeal that Silvia had been through. Unfortunately, she didn't receive counseling. He could only hope that she was emotionally in a place where there were no side effects.

He stretched out across the bed and watched TV, as she showered. He could hear her singing as she bathed. Well, she seems to be in a good place, he thought to himself; yet he remained a little uncertain.

Silvia, on the other hand, was definitely in a good place! She'd never been happier. Nate was quite shocked, as she burst through the door. There she stood, in her long satin white gown, with the hair in an updo ponytail. Just the sight of her made his heart race. There was no doubt about it, he was in love with this woman!

"Okay, Papi, it's babytime!" She yelled as she dived into the bed, landing right on top of him.

"Wait, wait—what?" asked Nate, laughing, throwing her off him at the same time.

"Wait, babe, let me get some clarification! What are you talking about, babytime?"

"Well, I've been thinking, and think we should get this baby train moving! I mean, you are 10 years older than I am. I want my babies to have memories of their father running, playing and chasing them. Not memories of him in a wheelchair! I want to give you a son to raise and a daughter to spoil."

All this hit Nate like a ton of bricks! He was

speechless.

"Wow, honey, you really know how to set the mood. I totally understand and agree with what you are saying; it's just that, I wasn't expecting you to come out here in baby mode! Forgive me if I seem a little shocked. Well, now that we are on the same page, "baby mode" it is! However, you know that it's nearly impossible that you will conceive, tonight.

Is there anything else you need to get off your mind or heart?" asked Nate sarcastically.

"Nope," Sylvia replied.

"Then get over here..."

It had been a few weeks since the wedding and both couples were settling into their new lives together, as man and wife. Early one Saturday morning, Nate decided to try his hand in the kitchen. A little breakfast in bed sounded like a good idea!

Just as he started the coffee maker, he was startled by a desperate banging on the front door.

"Who is it?" he yelled.

"Nema," replied the voice on the other side of the door.

It was Arkarma's next door neighbor's child.

"Nema! What in the world are you doing out here, child?" asked Nate, dragging her inside the house. "What's wrong?"

"Mama and Mrs. Arkarma sent me to get Mrs. Silvia! It's the baby! The baby is coming, but they need help!"

"OK, OK, hold on, we're coming. I'll take you

back, it's still dark outside!" Nate yelled as he raced towards the bedroom.

"Silvia! Silvia, baby, wake up!" he yelled, shaking her frantically.

"What? What's wrong, Papi?"

"Arkarma's in labor and they need you! They sent little Nema to come get you, cell service is bad over there! So come on, let's go!"

Silvia threw back the covers, ran to the dresser, grabbed her muumuu and slipped it on.

"OK, I'm ready!"

"Ummm, what's that?" Nate asked, eyeing her garb.

"It's my muumuu. One of the bridesmaids made it for me. She said that every woman should have a muumuu, for cases of emergency."

OK..." he replied, thinking that it looked more like an old quilt!

"Come on, man, there's no time to be discussing attire—babies come here naked," said Silvia.

As they headed out the door, she grabbed her black bag and threw a few things in it that she might need. She'd spent the last six months helping Lupe's sister in the Hills. She was now an experienced midwife, with thirty-three successful deliveries under her belt. Within seconds, a horn was blowing at the front door. Nate pulled out his Hummer. It rained a few hours earlier which meant the old dirt road was probably bad. Nevertheless, Nate drove like a madman! It was only a fourth of a mile, but it seemed longer and they felt every pothole along the way.

Silvia couldn't imagine how the child rode a bike in the dark, on the muddy road. They drove up to the cottage to find Dhunganda pacing on the front porch! He was a bag of nerves!

"Well, well, brother, looks like this is it! You're about to be a daddy!" Nate jived him.

"Yes man, it's crazy! I'm afraid for my wife right now, she's been hurting for a minute! Before she didn't want me to leave her side... now she's kicking me out!"

"Your wife is very hormonal, uncomfortable and irritable right now. Don't take it personal," Silvia explained. Then, she ran to her best friend's bedside.

"Silvia!" Arkarma cried when she saw her friend. A small wave of relief rushed across her face.

"I can see the fear in your eyes. Don't worry, you got this! Relax, I'm here! Now let's get my baby niece or nephew into this world!" said Silvia, encouraging her friend.

Arkarma moaned, as another contraction rippled through her body.

"Ok, please get some hot water and clean towels ready," Silvia shouted to Nema's mom. "Yep, the baby is definitely crowning; it won't be long." With each contraction, Arkarma pushed, yelled, screamed and moaned!

"I can't take this, I should be in there!" said Dhunganda, in desperation.

"No, you probably should wait out here!" Nate advised.

Suddenly, they were blinded by the bright lights of another vehicle approaching the cottage.

"What's going on? Is Arkarma in labor?" asked Mama Joyce, calling through the passenger-side window.

"I knew it! I knew it," said Lupe, climbing out of the car as quickly as possible.

"How did you know that something was going on?" asked Nate.

"I woke up in a cold sweat. I dreamed that I was holding a freshly delivered baby in my hands, goo and all! I told Mama about it, so we decided to come see if everything was OK; and now look, we're having a baby!"

After several pushes at Silvia's demand, Arkarma was exhausted. Once more Silvia checked her cervix, only to find that the baby was not moving down the birth canal. Something was wrong! The baby appeared to be stuck.

"I can't, I can't push anymore!" said Arkarma, crying.

Silvia also realized that Arkarma's face was getting pale.

"What are we going to do?" whispered Mama Joyce.

"I know what to do," said Silvia. "Nate! Nate!" she yelled. "Ladies, cover her up! Wrap the blanket around her like a burrito! Nate! Nate!" she yelled again.

"Wait, why is she calling for you, and not me?" asked Dhunganda.

Seeing that his friend was offended, Nate pretended that he didn't hear Silvia calling him.

Suddenly the door swung open. "Nate—Nate, I need you!" This time, he recognized the fear in her voice and knew that something was wrong.

Before he could take his first step, "Nathaniel, get in here!" rang from Arkarma's bedroom.

"OMG, that's mama!" said Nate. "Come on, Dhunganda, you go first!"

Not knowing what to expect, the men cautiously entered the bedroom.

Dhunganda was surprised to see his wife looking so ill.

"What's wrong? Why is she so pale?" he asked, frightened.

"Babe, pick her up and take her down the hill to the big tree!" Silvia ordered.

"Outside?" everyone questioned at the same time.

"Yes, outside!" Mama Joyce, grab those towels and another clean blanket, please ... Let's go, guys, now!"

Everyone quickly sprang into action. It was barely daylight. Nate scooped Arkarma into his arms and scurried quickly down the hill. It reminded him of rescuing Silvia; now she was the love of his life! Nate stopped at the base of the hill and waited for directions. Silvia spread the blanket onto the ground under the big oak tree, then pointed. Nate gently lowered Arkarma onto the blanket and took a step back. Mama Joyce took the other blanket from Dhunganda.

"I think you guys need to go back up the hill and wait. We will call for you once the baby is here," Silvia suggested.

Without questioning, they obeyed and proceeded back up the hill.

"OK, sweetie, come on, get down on your hands and knees," said Silvia. "Now, on your next contraction, reach up and grab the tree, spread your legs and push!"

"Are you sure?" Arkarma asked, doubtfully.

"Yes, I am, please just do it! We are going to let gravity help Mother Nature. Please trust me, sis..."

Mama Joyce and Nema's mom unwrapped her. It wasn't long before she was hit with another contraction.

"OK love, crawl close to the tree, grab it and hold on! Squat and push!" Silvia ordered, yelling like a sergeant in the military. Arkarma did exactly as she was told, but the baby did not move! Another contraction hit. "Push, girl, push!" Silvia yelled.

"Oh God, I'm so tired, I feel like I'm going to pass out," Arkarma mumbled.

"Dhunganda! Dhunganda, come…now! shouted Silvia.

Silvia's beckoning scared him and interrupted his prayer. Dhunganda ran down the hill, his heart in his throat. Arkarma didn't look good at all. She was barely hanging on.

Silvia, meanwhile, was focused and authoritative.

"Get down there! Get behind her, brace her and pray!" With Dhunganda behind her, Arkarma gave one last push, and … it worked! Gravity and Mother Nature gently got the baby onto the folded blanket. The women quickly ordered Dhunganda back up the hill! He really didn't want to go, but with tears of joy in his eyes, he obeyed. Nate met him, as he approached the top of the hill.

"Jeez, man, what happened?"

Before Dhunganda could answer, a faint baby's cry rang out into the morning silence.

"Thank you, Lord," said Nate.

The guys waited for their cue to return. Within a few minutes, they were summoned.

"Can you please take her back, honey?" Silvia requested.

Nate scooped Arkarma up, who was now wrapped in the clean blanket and carried her to the house.

"Here you are, daddy, now hurry up and get him inside before he gets cold."

"He? It's a boy?" asked Dhunganda. His legs buckled a little underneath him.

"Now, if you aren't able to carry him…" said Mama Joyce.

"No ma'am, I got him," said the proud father.

"Well, tuck him close and get him inside!" she ordered.

The baby had been swaddled in towels. Dhunganda unzipped his jacket and tucked his son inside. Within seconds, he was in the house. Silvia helped Arkarma get settled and then they all left the little happy family alone.

Silvia was so tired, she fell asleep in the car. Nate didn't wake her. He picked her up, carried her inside and laid her on the couch. He loved carrying her and thanked God for every opportunity. He laid her on the bed and rushed into the shower.

We are still newlyweds. I want to spend time loving and learning about my wife first, he thought to himself. He couldn't believe that he was wondering what it would be like if they had a baby. Just as he was getting out of the shower, there was a knock on the door.

Papi, are you finished? Please don't use all that water!"

He wrapped his towel around him and opened the door. It's all yours, ma'am, I saved you some hot water."

"Thanks, love," she said, giving him a peck on the lips. Just as he exited the door, she snatched his towel and quickly locked the door!

"Silvia!"

She laughed uproariously in reply.

"You have to come back out here sooner or later...I'll be waiting!" threatened Nate, laughing.

For the next few weeks, Arkarma received the royal treatment. Between Sylvia, Mama Joyce, and her family from the Hills, she had around-the-clock help. Nannys, cooks and maids were at her beck and call.

One day, Aunt Paca came to visit. She took one look at Silvia and knew that she was pregnant.

"Come here, honey," she invited, sitting in the rocking chair. "Hold your head back, please..." Silvia did as she was told. She knew exactly what Aunt Paca was looking for. She took two fingers and placed them on Silvia's throat. "Yep, just like I thought, there's a second heartbeat. She's pregnant! One thing old Paca knows is a pregnant woman when she sees one!

"Child, go lay across Arkarma's bed and let me check you." Silvia laid across the bed and pulled up her shirt. "Silvia baby, you're probably about eight weeks."

Eight weeks?" Silvia thought. "That would mean we conceived on or around our wedding night! OMG, I've got to go tell my husband!"

When she returned home, she found Nate stretched out on the couch.

"Babe, what are you doing home so early?" she asked.

"I feel sick, really icky! I think I'm coming down with something," complained Nate.

Silvia stood deep in thought. She'd been about to tell him the good news, but now she was thinking about saving it until his birthday next month. She was curious to know how much of a "big baby" God had blessed her with.

"Silv, babe...did you hear me?"

"Oh yes, Papi, I heard you. I'll tell you what, go lie down for a while. I will bring you some freshly squeezed orange juice and a couple of aspirins."

"I hope that I'm not catching some type of bug..." he mumbled.

You've got a bug alright, she thought, smiling.

Silvia soon entered the bedroom to find Nate in bed, having cold sweats. He didn't want the juice or aspirins.

"Babe, something's wrong. I'm having chills in the summertime; I don't understand.

I mean, I've been sick before, but I've never felt like this."

Silvia felt so guilty. She knew that it was time to tell him.

"OK, Nate, please take these aspirins and move over. I'm going to get in bed with you."

"I don't know about that, babe—this thing might be contagious! I think we really should go to the doctor."

"No, my love, in a few days you will be just fine," she said, trying to restrain her laughter.

It was sad, yet so cute! Reluctantly, he did as she had advised.

Silvia pulled back the covers and crawled in beside him. The poor thing was sweating like a pig and his skin was cold and clammy.

"Maybe we should just call my mama," Nate suggested.

She scooted in and threw her arms around him, trying to provide some body heat. Lord knows, she had enough of it! She was pregnant and under the covers in 110-degree weather!

"No, my love, I don't think that even your mother could help you with this one," she whispered.

"What? You act as if you know what's wrong with me!"

"I do," she replied.

"What is it? Do I have some kind of bug or something? Come on, babe...tell me, I feel like I'm dying here."

She laughed. "Nope, Nate, surely you shall live and not die. You have been bitten by the love bug, baby. Actually, we both have...feel this."

She took his hand and rubbed it across the bottom of her abdomen.

"Do you feel that little bulge?"

Too shocked to answer, he just laid there. So, Silvia continued.

"You have been bitten by the "daddy bug". You have what most men get, when his woman is pregnant. Surely you have heard of it?"

"Yes, I have...I just never had it! ...Are you sure?"

"Yes, husband, I'm sure."

"But we just got married," said Nate.

"Yep, and who said that it wasn't likely that we'd conceive on our honeymoon? If I have calculated correctly, it was on or shortly after we returned home."

"Actually, we are still on our honeymoon," he added.

"Are you happy?"

"What? Am I happy? If I weren't so cold, weak

and wet I'd be doing cartwheels!"

"Whew, you had me scared for a moment there," said Silvia.

"Now, you know that's one thing that you never have to be with me, is scared," said Nate.

"Well good then, with all of that said…you'll understand if I left this one for you. I'm burning up! Between my hormones, the baby and this heat, I have to go! So tough it out, soldier, you're going to be fine!"

Silvia threw back the covers and sprang out of the bed.

"Be back to check on you soon, Papi!"

"OK, babe. OMG, I'm going to be a dad!" he said to himself, smiling under the covers.

Within a couple of days, Nate was over the "daddy bug" and was in full force daddy mode! He was making plans to build a crib, turn Mama Joyce's old room into a nursery, etc. etc. etc.

"Nate, my abuela said that you should never make too many plans for a baby. Wait until you are at least six weeks; then it's safe to make plans and tell people that you're actually pregnant."

"I understand, but I'm not worried. The fruit of your womb is blessed. I pray over you and our baby every night."

"Thank you, my covering."

"She's going to be just fine," proclaimed Nate confidently.

"How do you know that it's a girl?"

"I just know," said Nate.

"Nope. I disagree, it's a boy. I'm sure of it, and his name is Santiago."

"Well, I say that it's a girl, and her name is Madeline. We will call her Maddie."

"Well, I guess we will see, Papi!"

"I guess we will, my love."

Time passed, and Silvia's baby grew rapidly. She continued to deliver babies, until her own big day. One morning, she woke up with a desperate urge to use the bathroom. She'd been cramping all night but refused to tell Nate. As she sat on the toilet she felt pressure. She reached down, only to feel the baby's head!

"NATE! Nathaniel! Nathaniel, come here! Veni aqui Papi, anjali!"

Still half-asleep, Nate heard her calling. He knew enough Spanish to understand that she'd said come here quickly! He staggered into the bathroom.

"Papi, look," she said, spreading her legs.

"No, I don't want to..."

"Nathaniel, look!" she snapped.

Against his will, Nate took a peep. "Is that my baby?"

"Yes! Now go to the linen closet and get some clean towels and blankets. Then, get the pillows off our bed," she ordered.

"Do you want me to boil some water too?" he asked.

"No, Nate—please go, and hurry!"

Nate made it back just in time for a contraction. "Put the blankets in the tub and help me in. We're doing this together," she said, grimacing from the pain.

"'We', as in meaning you and me? By ourselves? With no help? Wait, baby, let me get my cell phone and call my mama," Nate pleaded as he helped her into the tub.

"Nope, you can call her after we're done," she said, moaning.

"But what if something goes wrong?"

"It won't! I'm a midwife!" she yelled through the contraction. "If it makes you feel better, go get the phone and put it on the sink. Hurry!"

Jesus, Jesus, Jesus! Lord, please help me! begged Nate as he returned with the phone.

"Baby. are you sure you want to do this…this way? I'm not cut out for this!"

"Honey, you're a soldier, for Pete's sake! You're cut out for everything! Wash your hands and get ready!" Every time she had a contraction, Silvia began to speak in Spanish and Nate spoke in his heavenly language.

The third contraction came, and Silvia began to push.

"Oh Lord, I think I have to pee now," said Nate, kneeling and quaking beside the tub.

"Shut up, Nate, and guide this baby out!" she snapped.

Together, Nate and Silvia gave birth to their first-born, a baby girl they decided to call Maddie.

As soon as mom and baby were settled in bed, Nate raced back to the bathroom to wash his hands and grab his cell phone.

Mama Joyce picked up on the third ring! "Ma, I need you to come now! Silvia and I just had the baby!" he yelled. Before she could say one word, he hung up the phone. Then, he went to relieve himself.

"Lord, have mercy! I'm never using this bathroom again," he mumbled.

"Oh, Nate...you can calm down now, come and get your daughter," Silva laughed. "So what do you think?"

"OMG, she's a redhead!" exclaimed Nate.

"What?"

"What I meant was...I haven't met too many red head Hispanics. So if she has the red hair like my mother and the salsa flair of her mother, I might be in trouble! No, seriously, she's beautiful, an angel, my love."

"I think she already has her daddy's heart. By the way, did I forget to mention to you that my mom has red hair? Guess Maddie's going to have a triple dose of flair!"

"I don't care, she's still going to be 'daddy's girl'". Nate's heart filled with joy as he gazed down at his baby girl. "Let's pray over her," he suggested.

He reached into his nightstand and pulled out a little valve of oil. He anointed himself, Silvia and the baby. Then he prayed, thanking God for his family. Suddenly, there was a pounding on the front door; it was Mama Joyce.

"Nate! Nate, come open this door!" she yelled.

"Yep, that's your grandma..." he said to Maddie, before handling her back to her mom.

"Where is she?" demanded Mama Joyce, almost pushing him down, trying to get inside. "Well, good morning, mother," he said as she marched by.

"Oh, Silvia darling," she whined as she walked into the room and saw her daughter-in-law holding her first grandchild. Tears began to roll down her face.

"Mama Joyce, meet your granddaughter Maddie," said Silvia, as she handed the baby over.

She also gestured for Lupe to enter the room. He too came over to see the tiny, little angel.

"Isn't she precious, and she's a redhead," Lupe added.

"That's what Nate said," replied Silvia, laughing.

"Oh...she might be a little whippersnapper!"

"That's not always true," Mama Joyce chimed in. "Look at me!"

"You're right, love, thank you for the spice that you bring to my life," he said, planting a kiss on her cheek.

"Oh, stop it, Lupe; we are too old to be thinking about another baby." "Ok, I'm feeling sick again..." said Nate.

"Well, I'm going to go get Paca, so she can come see about you properly," said Lupe.

"Thanks, Uncle Lupe," Silvia replied.

"I'm going with you," Nate said. "After all that I've been through, I could use a little fresh air! I'll be back in a second, babe, Mama's going to take care of you, okay?"

"Yes, husband. You were so brave and you did a good job! I'm so proud of you, Papi."

"Was he really brave? I thought he would have been scared," whispered Mama Joyce as soon as Nate walked out of the room.

"Oh Mom, he was super chicken, freaking out! I had to remind him that he was a soldier!" They both laughed.

Nate sat quietly, looking out of the window as Lupe drove.

"So how was it?" Lupe asked, smiling.

"I don't want to talk about it. All I can say is, it was memorable and I'm not using that tub again, for a very long time!"

"You'll get over it," said Lupe, smiling.

Just as predicted, Maddie grew up to be a daddy's girl! She stole his heart the moment he laid eyes on her. As soon as she could walk, she became his shadow. She loved her daddy!

Nate held to his word and didn't use the tub for about a year. Just when he became comfortable with his bathroom again, Silvia made the big announcement at the Christmas brunch.

"Oh Nate, I forgot to give you this gift. I left it in my purse," said Silvia, handing him a nicely wrapped package.

"Are you sure that it's for me? It's kind of small," he said sarcastically, accepting the gift.

"Oh, it's bigger than you think," she replied.

By now, all eyes were on Nate and the mystery gift.

"What? For me? Really, are you sure?" Nate questioned, as he pulled out a small pair of baby booties.

"Oh sweetie, I do this for a living. I'm sure brother…we are pregnant!" she laughed.

"Well, I was saving some news until later, myself." Arkarma turned to Dhunganda, took his hand, placed it on her belly, and said his name.

"What babe, you too? You're pregnant too? OMG!"

"Well, Merry Christmas to everyone!" said Lupe, laughing.

"Well, all I'm going to say is…I'm just getting back into my bathroom. This time, Silvia, you and Arkarma will be there down there by the tree together! Dhunganda and I will wait at the top of the hill!"

"Nate!" said everyone simultaneously.

"What? I'm just teasing," said Nate as he looked at Dhunganda, making "OMG, I don't believe this" eyes at each other!

"This time it's going to be a boy!" announced Nate.

"Oh, here we go again," laughed Silvia.

Silvia and Arkarma enjoyed being pregnant together. They took evening strolls, swapped ideas and got fat together. They even compared bellies.

"Nothing like being pregnant with your sister," Arkarma said contentedly.

"Nope, and nothing like watching the guys squirm together," Silvia replied mischievously.

They both laughed.

Maddie and Anyo grew up like sisters and brothers. Having to share their parents with the new babies came quite as a surprise. Arkarma and Silvia both gave birth to bouncing baby boys.

Arkarma named her son Miko. Silvia named her baby Santiago. Aunt Paca delivered them both and life was well on the Outback. How time flew. Santiago and Miko grew like little weeds. Maddie slowly lost her tomboyish ways, when she was in high school. She now depended on Silvia to help her become lady-like.

One evening, Arkarma's cousin from the Hills came to visit.

"Who's that?" asked Silvia, as a strange car pulled up into Arkarma's driveway.

The car door opened slowly and to Arkarma's surprise, it was one of her cousins from the Hills.

"Nola!"

She recognized her immediately. The two cousins ran to greet each other. Slowly, the back door opened and a young man emerged.

"Do you remember Rodriguez, we call him Rico?"

"Yes, I remember little Rico. He and Anyo are around the same age. Come on; let me introduce you to my sister and best friend, Silvia." The three women had a nice chat as the smaller children played. Anyo introduced Rico to Maddie and the two gave him a tour of the farm.

"Rico, Rico, Rico! Silvia, who is Rico?" asked Nate that night.

"Oh, he is one of Arkarma's cousins from the Hills; why?"

"Because I'm getting tired of hearing that name! He's the only thing that Maddie has been talking about since yesterday!"

"Easy, Daddy, I think your daughter has her first boy crush!"

"Boy crush? She's too young to be thinking about boys!"

"She's not, Nate! She's in high school!"

"Yeah, well, I heard that he was a 'bad boy', right?"

"Well, I won't say that he's a 'bad boy', but he could use a little guidance," observed Silvia.

"Well, I'm glad that he's gone!"

"Don't be too overprotective, Nate!"

The next day, Nola came back and spoke with Arkarma and Dhunganda.

"Cousin, I need a huge favor. Well, Rico has been following the wrong crowd in the Hills. We are afraid these people are going to be a bad influence on him. Not only that, Rod and I have fallen on hard times. We were wondering if you guys could take him in for the summer? He needs to get away, to experience another type of lifestyle. Besides—honestly, we can't feed him. Maybe get him a job at the mill? I heard that is doing well, down here."

CHAPTER SEVEN

"Yeah, well, it's doing pretty good, but we don't normally hire teenagers," said Dhunganda.

"Let us talk it over and we will let you know tomorrow."

Together, they decided not to hire him at the mill, but they agreed to let him stay for the summer, to give his parents a break. ddie rejoiced over the news.

Nate, on the other hand, hated it.

"I swear, I can't wait until the summer is over! We have to find something for Maddie to do around here! I don't like her hanging out with the boys all day."

"Well, she gets up and does her chores...what do you want me to do with her, lock her in her room all day?"

"That's an idea!"

"Oh, for Pete's sake, Nate!"

"I just don't trust that Rico fella at all!"

"Well, I'm sure Anyo won't let anything happen to Maddie, honey. She's the only sister he's ever known. I'm pretty sure he'd protect her with his life."

"Now there's a vote of confidence, Silv, he's nerdy and scrawny. I'd put my bucks on Maddie defending herself!"

"I'm gonna teach her some self-defense moves."

"OK Daddy," Silvia said, thinking, he talks about Rico just as much as Maddie does …

By the end of summer, Rico and Maddie were in the throes of puppy love. She cried for two days straight when he went back home to the Hills.

Nate, on the other hand, rejoiced! He was singing and everything.

"Oh please, Mr. Brodgen, don't rejoice in your daughter's heartache, said Silvia. "Can't you at least pretend to feel sorry for your daughter?"

"OK, I will have a talk with my princess, Nate said, feeling somewhat rotten. He went into her room, to find Maddie sitting in the corner, on the floor polishing her nails.

"Hey, my love," he said, announcing himself as he entered. "I wanted to talk to you about Rico. I know that you're very fond of him and his leaving seems to have you in the dumps. Just know, you're a beautiful young lady and there will be other young men to come into your life."

"Oh, I'm a little sad, but I'm not too sad. Rico gave me a promise ring—look," Maddie said, flashing a little plastic ring. "He promised to come back for me. He should be back next summer. So I'm good, Daddy, don't worry about me."

"Yeah, well, that's almost impossible to do, princess." He gave her a little kiss on her forehead. Then, he left the room.

Nate came back into the living room, furious. He flopped down into his recliner chair.

"So how did it go?" Silvia asked.

"Not good, not good at all. That little sucker is a step ahead of me. He gave her a promise ring!"

"Aww!"

Nate gave her the evil eye. "I think this boy just may be a problem!"

"Hopefully not," Silvia countered.

The next summer, Maddie was sadly disappointed. Rico did not return, and neither did he bother to write.

"What's going on with Rico?" Silvia asked Arkarma.

"I don't know, but I intend to find out. My niece is so sad. I hate seeing her like this! She hasn't even been hanging out with Anyo," Arkarma noted.

"Nope, she's just been shut up in her room," Silvia confirmed.

Arkarma called her cousin Nova and found out that Rico was working for a local picking and delivering peaches.

Later that afternoon, Silvia told Maddie the bad news. She suggested that she too find a job for the summer. "Tomorrow, why don't we ladies take a trip to the square? Mama Joyce can keep the babies. Arkarma and I can shop, while you job hunt."

"Sounds wonderful," agreed Maddie. "What time shall we leave?"

"Well, let me set everything up first and then I'll

let you know." Silvia was relieved to see the enthusiasm in her child's face again.

Mama Joyce and Lupe enjoyed their new life together. Every day was an adventure. Mama Joyce was slightly younger than Lupe, and full of energy. "Hey Lupe, let's go fishing!" she said one day.

"Mama, we already have more fish than the freezer can hold," Lupe replied.

"I know, but there's something about fishing that is so relaxing. I love it when the fish are biting."

"OK love, we'll go when it cools off this evening. I will tell you what: if we keep catching fish like we have, then we might have to sell them."

"Lupe, that's a good idea. We can start a fish market. You were talking about how the fish in the creek are overpopulating, because of the dam that the beavers built."

"Yeah, I did, Mama, but we're going to need a building and that's just too much!

No! We can have our business here. All we need is a long stand or two. We will give it a try," said Lupe.

"Great, I will get some worms." Lupe had taught Joyce how to find the black dirt with the worms. She went under one of the trees, flipped over a large piece of tin and wrigglers were everywhere! "Look at you! It's amazing, Mama, when you first got here, you wouldn't touch a worm or fish. Now, I can't keep you away from either!"

"Guess the Outback way of life is wearing me down," grinned Mama Joyce. They went fishing, returning with about 30 fish. They went home and put them on ice in a large cooler. Lupe put a sign out by the road, "Mama Lupe's Fresh Fish". In less than an hour, they were sold out. Nate was their last, happy customer.

The girls' trip was a welcome thought. Nate agreed that it would be a good idea to get Maddie out of the house, and her mind off that Rico boy. The square was super busy. It was harvest time and everyone had something to sell.

"Mom, I want to walk over to the other side for a minute. I would love to get some perfume and see if anyone's hiring," said Maddie.

"OK, honey. I will meet you at the Porta-Potty in 15 minutes."

"Sure, Mommy," said Maddie as she ran towards the perfume. As soon as she was out of sight, she v-lined and exited the square.

Rico had shown her which jalopy he rode to get to the Hills. With her money in her hands, she was determined to go find him!

"Can you take me to the Hills, please?".

"What part?"

"Nunes. I'm looking for the Arnold family. Rico is my boyfriend."

"Rico, yeah I know Rico. Come on," said the gentleman.

Maddie climbed the back of the old truck full of people. She had just enough room to squeeze in by the tailgate. "You know it's going to be $6," said the gentleman.

"Yes, I know," she responded.

The ride was long and bumpy. After about 15 minutes, she looked at her watch. She knew her mom was hysterical by now!

Back at the square, Silvia was crying. "I'm going to have to call Nate, it's almost dark and there's no sign of Maddie anywhere!"

The square was almost empty, as most people had packed up and gone home. They'd searched over and over. There was no sign of Maddie.

"I told her to meet me here at the Porta-Potty! I don't know what happened," wailed Silvia, still crying.

"OK girl, try to remain as calm as possible. Give me the phone and I'll call Nate," Arkarma offered.

Nate picked up on the first ring. "Silvia! Why haven't you been answering my calls?"

"It's me, Arkarma, Nate."

"Oh, where is Silvia and Maddie?" he asked.

"Well, Silvia is right here and that's why I'm calling...Nate, can you come to the square? We can't find Maddie!"

"WHO? You what?" he yelled.

"Try to remain calm, but—no, we can't find her anywhere and Silvia is on the edge of a panic attack!"

"So am I! OK, I'm on my way! But first, let me speak to Silvia!"

"Hello, Nate! Babe, I can't find her anywhere! I can't find my baby, Maddie is missing!"

"OK love, I'm on my way! You and Arkarma go

sit in the truck until I get there, it's almost dark."

"Dark." That's exactly what Maddie was thinking, as she bounced up the mountain. No wonder they called it the hills! There was one time when she thought that they would fall off the narrow road. It didn't help that they frequently stopped, letting people off. It was almost dark, with only her and two men left. "Excuse me, how much longer do we have to get to Nunes?"

"It's the last stop; we should get there shortly after dark." The man could see the fear and frustration on her face. "Who are you going to see in Nunes?"

"My friend—I'm going to see Rico."

The man smiled and then chuckled, shaking his head. "I'm Rico's dad. What's your name, youngin?"

"Maddie," she responded.

"Gladiator's daughter? Yep, heard all about you! My boy was working down there, this past summer. What are you, coming to see him?"

"Yes," she replied.

"Does Nola know that you are coming?"

"Well no, she doesn't. I was…"

"You were just going to pop up! So, I guess this means that Gladiator doesn't know that you're gone. I was wondering why a youngin like yourself would be out this late, all alone. Do you know that we have coyotes and bears in these parts? The boy's mom and me are feuding right now. I guess I have no choice but to take you over there. Gladiator is a good man; we don't want no trouble with him."

By the time the conversation ended, the truck had

come to a halt. OK missy, that's us, let's go!" As they walked, Maddie realized it really had been a bad idea of hers. She really didn't know the man that she was walking with or where he was taking her. But it was dark and she had no one else. They walked a couple of yards up the road.

"Do you see how unsafe this was, sweetie? It's almost pitch-black dark out here."

"Yes sir, I should have thought it through," Maddie agreed wholeheartedly.

As they approached the driveway, Maddie's stomach dropped. She wanted to see Rico so bad, but now she really knew that this idea was crazy!

His dad knocked on the door and Nola opened it.

"Wait, before you get started...this ain't about me! We got a little situation here and I have a little package for you." Reaching behind him, he led Maddie into the doorway. "This is Gladiator's daughter! I found her on the jalopy by herself, coming up here to see Rico."

"Yes, I know exactly who she is; my Lord, child, what were you thinking? Rod, get her in here, while I call Arkarma."

Arkarma picked up on the second ring. "Hey cousin, let me call you back, I'm kind of busy right now," she said. "I know, busy looking for Maddie, right?" asked Nola.

"Yes, how did you know about it?"

"Arkarma, she's fine; Maddie is here!"

"She is what?"

"Yes, Rod happened to find her coming up on the last jalopy. You know it doesn't get here until after dark! He was concerned and found out that she was looking for Rico."

"OK cousin, we are on our way!"

Nate had walked the whole square three times searching everywhere he could think of. He stopped and questioned the few people that he saw; there was no sign of her. Silvia walked slowly, crying at his side. He knew that he had to be strong for her. It took all that he had to force back the tears welling up inside of him.

After receiving the news, Arkarma jumped into the Hummer and started blowing the horn. Nate, Silvia and Dhunganda, who had joined them, came running.

"Guys, stop looking! Stop looking for her, she's fine! I just got a call from Nola—she has Maddie. Apparently, she dissed us and caught the last jalopy into the hills.

"She did what? That thing arrives way after dark!" Nate yelled.

"Yes, Rico's dad happened to find her and took her to Nola."

"Thank God," exhaled Nate.

Silvia broke out in sobs of relief! "I know what you were thinking, although Lou said it was impossible. I can't say that the same thought didn't cross my mind," confessed Nate. "We can dismiss it now! Once again, God has answered our prayers. It's not by coincidence that she was on the jalopy with Rod.

"However, it does make me just dislike that Rico kid even more! What was Maddie thinking? She's going to be on punishment until she's 80 years old!"

Just as they were about to leave, Nate looked at his wife. Then he looked at Arkarma, and changed his mind.

"Dhunganda, we have a change of plans, bro. Our wives are beat, they're tired. All I want is to see my child right now. However, we both know those roads to the Hills are narrow and winding. It's too rough and dangerous for us to attempt at night. It's best that we camp out at the hillside B&B and go get her in the morning. I will pay for everything."

"Sounds like a winner, I will personally call Nola when I get in the truck. Don't worry, she'll be sleeping with Nola; Uncle Dhunganda's orders! She's my only daughter too!"

"Thanks bro," said Nate, touched.

The B&B was beautiful. They all got some well-needed rest. The owner, Miss Sadie, gave Gladiator a discount for his service. Right after breakfast, they were on their way.

"These Hills roads are quite bumpy!" groaned Silvia.

"It's all part of living off the grid. Why don't you let your seat back, it might be a little more comfortable," Nate suggested.

"OK," Sylvia replied.

The ride was quite intense. Nate was having mixed emotions; anxious and grateful to get his baby girl back. Yet, on the other hand, he was furious that she made such a crazy and deceitful decision!

Rico and Maddie stayed up most of the night, talking. She wanted answers.

"Maddie, I can't believe you ran away and came up here all alone! Do you have any idea how dangerous that was?"

"No, I didn't at that time. I wasn't thinking straight. I've been writing to you and you haven't replied to any of my letters. You didn't come down for the summer as promised! I wanted to know what was up. I even had Anyo call you. You didn't return his call, either. You even look different...act different. What's the deal?"

"Maddie, that wild boy...Rico, from last summer, is gone. Things aren't good around here. People are losing their jobs; Dad was one of them. Then, he started drinking. He and Mom were fighting, even talking about getting a divorce. I had to step up and grow up fast! I sold my bike and got a job, to help Mom catch up on bills...and we're still struggling. I'm sorry that I hurt you. I know that I promised to come back, but I couldn't sit here idle while my whole world was falling apart. I had to choose between staying a boy and being a man. My mom needed me. Hope that you understand."

"Maddie could only sit there in disbelief! Here it was, his whole world was crumbling, while she was having attention tantrums! The hurt and anguish was all over his face.

"Rico, I'm so sorry; I feel so stupid! Tell you what, let me talk to my dad. Maybe you guys can move down there with us." "Really, Maddie? Your dad hates me!"

"He does not, he's just a little overprotective. However, he does his own lumber company; maybe he can give your dad a job.

"Do you really think that he would help us? He thinks I'm the reason you ran away!"

"I got this! No matter how much my dad looks like a grizzly, I know his heart. I will talk to him. God knows I'm going to have plenty of time to do it. I'm going to be on punishment until eternity!"

It was morning and Rico was up at dawn. He wanted to be out of the house before Nate arrived. He quietly tiptoed into his mom's room and gave her a light kiss on the forehead. Then he went to Maddie's side of the bed. He planted a light kiss on her forehead as well, but left his lips there just a little bit longer. He looked up, only to find his mom staring back into his eyes. He winked at her and quickly made an exit!

Finally, the bumpy road trip ended! Dhunganda pulled his truck in front of the house and stopped. Nate followed suit.

"Now Nate, please don't get in here and go gladiator on 'em. Remember that it was our daughter that ran away. Rico had nothing to do with it," Silvia pointed out

Nate closed his eyes and took a deep breath. "OK love, come on—let's go get her."

Nola and Maddie were eating breakfast when

they arrived. Nate chose to stay silent and let Silvia do the talking. He didn't have to say a word. His aura and disposition screamed that he was enraged! It was a look that Maddie had never seen before. It scared her to the very core of her being. She was glad that Rico wasn't home.

"Nova, I can't tell you how grateful we are, to you and your husband. We were scared out of our minds!"

"I can't imagine! You're welcome, and for the first time, Rico was innocent," she pointed out.

"Yes, we know. We appreciate everything; if there's anything that we can do for you, just let us know."

"Well, actually there is," Maddie chimed in.

"Daddy, can you give Rico's dad a job at the mill? He lost his job and work here is slow."

Surprised and slightly embarrassed, Nova put in quickly, "No, no Maddie, he doesn't have to do that."

"Does he need work?" asked Nate.

"Yes."

"Then he's hired. Where is he?"

"A couple doors down the road."

"Can you call him? I'd like to meet him."

"Sure." Lord, I hope he's not drunk, Nola thought.

Within minutes, Rod burst through the door. "Hello Gladiator, nice to meet you again. I'm Rodriguez. They call me Rod," he said, with an extended hand.

"OK, Rod, I truly wanted to thank you for

145

protecting my daughter and seeing that she was safe. I know it had to be dark when the jalopy got here last night."

"Indeed it was. I told her how dangerous her decision was."

"Maddie tells me that you're in need of employment. If you're willing to relocate, I would like to offer you a position at the mill," Nate went on.

"Yes, yes, sir, I'll take it—whatever it is, Mr. Gladiator, I'll do it."

"You're welcome, and you can call me Nate. Now, when can you start?"

"Today! I can start today, if you want me to."

"No, tomorrow is fine. I expect you to be there around 7 a.m."

"Yes sir, I'll be there!" Rod replied.

Nate was moved emotionally when he looked up and saw tears streaming down Nola's face. It was obvious that this family was in dire need. Nate loaded up his family and proceeded on the long, bumpy ride down the mountain. The tension in the truck was thick. Super thick!

Silvia returned to her reclined position. Maddie sat quietly and uncertain, as Nate drove with mixed emotions. He was happy that he could be a blessing to this family in need. Then, there was the situation with Maddie.

"Well, look at God!" said Maddie, out of nowhere. "Out of all this, someone got blessed. I guess it was God that led me up the mountain."

"Not another word, Madeline!" Nate snapped

Madeline, really? she thought. OMG, that confirmed that I'm in serious trouble!

"No, it was not God! God did not tell you to run away from your mother and catch a ride up the mountain...chasing after a little boy!" Nate was raging now. "However, it was God that had Rico's dad on the truck with you, watching over you. I will say, God is Sovereign enough that he will keep you even when you can't keep yourself! Even as we make foolish decisions, he's still right there. God will keep you, when you can't keep yourself! He has given us the best GPS that will ever exist! It's the Holy Spirit. The Holy Spirit is constantly leading us; that is, when we are listening. But being the gentleman that he is, God always gives us the option of free will.

"The Holy Spirit may tell you, 'don't go left'! He doesn't want you to go left, because he can see the pitfalls ahead. Instead, he may lead you to go right; seeing that the road ahead is smooth and blessed. But nope, we choose to go left, anyway...now we have to endure all of the snakes, potholes and bumps in the road! Meanwhile, the Holy Spirit is still there saying "recalculating"! He is constantly calculating our routes, to see that we make it to our expected end. The end that God predestined for us. Of course, it takes some people longer than others to get there. It's according to how much you listen to your Divine GPS."

"PREACH!" said Silvia.

"Now, I know your GPS told you not to go up that hill. So, it looks like Daddy is going to have to teach you a little more about recognizing the voice of God. Tonight, you will be recognizing the voice and hand of your father."

"Nate—no," said Silvia.

"No, ma'am, it is written, 'spare the rod spoil the child'! Punishment is good, but there are times when the Rod of Correction is necessary. Now if anybody has a problem with that...then they need to take it up with God! There is a difference between spanking and beating."

"Yes, I agree, love," Silvia replied.

The truck was quiet for a long time. No one said anything.

"We're at the bottom of the mountain now, won't be much longer," said Nate. "I'll stop at the square and grab us some fruit or something. You and the runaway can stay in the car."

"Maddie dropped her head. She knew she was in trouble; her father had never spanked her before! She knew that she had his heart. Although it may hurt, he wouldn't kill her. He loved her!

Once at home, Nate took Maddie into her room. It was brief but effective. Afterwards, he explained why he did what he did, showing her how their lives would have been forever ruined if something had happened to her. Looking at the tears in her daddy's eyes, Maddie decided she never wanted to disappoint him like that again. She only hoped that she could live up to the promise.

The next morning when Nate pulled up to the mill, Rod was waiting on the steps. Rod turned out to be a good employee. He lived with his cousins during the week and went home on the weekends. He was a fast learner and he worked very hard. He stayed late, worked overtime, whatever he needed to do, to show Nate how appreciative he was and how much he needed his job. One morning he was a few minutes late. The word on the yard was that Nate was requesting his presence in his office!

All kinds of thoughts began to run through his mind. He was only a few minutes late! It was his first offense; some guys were late every day! He was praying that he didn't lose his job. God, please don't let me get fired! How could he ever tell Nola, he thought.

With sweaty palms, Rod knocked on the office door.

"You can come in. Have a seat," said Nate. "I called you in because I have been watching you. I see how quickly you learned almost every station. It seems as if you get along well with the fellows, so I'm offering you a promotion to supervisor."

"Me? Rod asked in disbelief.

"Yes you, that's if you want the position."

"Oh yes, yes I want it!"

"Your pay will increase by $4 an hour and I'm going to let you keep one of the old company trucks, so you won't have to depend on a ride to work."

Overwhelmed by it all, Rod broke down in tears,

149

then began to sob. Here he was thinking that he was about to get fired.

"Man, I thank you, I thank you so much! You don't realize what you have done for me and my family! Only a few months ago we were on the verge of being evicted. My wife was becoming disappointed in me as a man. I even felt less than a man. I was a drunk and she was speaking of divorce. I truly thank you, Nate."

"No problem, the Lord has a way of working things out," Nate replied.

Just as Rodriguez was about to leave the office, Lupe met him at the door. "Just the man I was looking for," he said.

"You've been looking for me too?"

"Yes sir, I just met a man at the post office. He said that he has a doublewide mobile home that he wants to sell ASAP. He's asking $10,000.00. It's a fixer upper, but overall in good condition. He's moving to Europe!"

"Oh man, Lupe, I couldn't do it even if someone gave me $10,000. I don't have any land to put it on."

"Suppose I gave you some land?" Lupe suggested.

"Suppose I gave you $10,000?" said Nate.

"What? You guys, can't possibly be thinking of giving me that kind of money."

"Actually, it would be considered as a loan, I'd take it out of your check."

"And Nola is my niece; you guys have been struggling for a while now. I think that it's time for a change. You guys can have the back half acre, on the other side of me and Mama Joyce."

"So, it looks like you guys have already discussed this, huh?" said Rod.

"Basically," confirmed Nate, smiling.

"Guys, this is too much! It's too good, too fast! I'm feeling overwhelmed." Rodriguez sat down and cried. "Fellas, I don't know what to say!"

"'Thank you' would be nice," said Lupe.

"Yes, yes, thank you, thank you both," Rod said, wiping his tears.

"Now, take the rest of the day off. I think you have important business to take care of!"

"He will be here at 12:30," said Lupe to Nate.

"Good, I'll have a check ready, it'll be right here." Rodriguez stood at the door wondering what he could possibly have done to gain such favor. His heart was so full!

"Don't look like that bro, it's fine. It's all God, it's all his doing. I think it's funny how people pray for things and when God answers, they get scared. They feel like it's too good to be true. Just receive it, bro! There's nothing too hard for God."

"Amen," said Rod.

"Now go, get your wife, so we can get this home moved to your new property. You guys can stay with me and Mama tonight. We have to get this home set up ASAP. The seller leaves Monday morning. Get Nola down here, so she can show us where she wants it," Lupe ordered.

"Yes sir, leaving now!"

Rod raced to his work truck and proceeded up the hills. Overwhelmed by it all, he pulled over at the base of the mountain. There again, he cried and thanked God.

When he arrived at the house, he found Nola outside raking the front yard. Without saying a word, he marched towards her and kissed her, the way he did when they first got married. Slightly stunned, Nola's first instinct was to fuss at him. They still weren't on the best of terms. Then she saw them, the traces of his tears. He had been crying. But at the moment he was happy, smiling. She didn't understand.

"OK, are you going to tell me what's going on? You're acting like a mad man right now."

"No honey, not mad...blessed. Blessed and Highly Favored! I can't tell you the whole story right now. It means that we need to get down the hill. Go get your li'l dusty butt in the shower, I will fill you in."

A few minutes later, Nola was so overjoyed she could barely bathe. She cried and praised God in the shower.

"Come on honey, hurry—they are waiting on us. Your uncle says that he won't set the home up until you get there. It's yours. He wants to know where you want it and which direction you want to put it."

"Nola quickly slipped on a dress and they were in their way. She made him repeat the story

several times. Nola left a note for Rico to stay with the neighbors. They would be back for him in the morning.

Silvia heard the news and was floored! She couldn't believe Nate did such a nice thing. Especially knowing that this meant Rico would live less than two miles away. The transition was smooth. Nate and Lupe helped Rod with the repairs as the ladies took care of the TLC the house needed.

Lupe also gave Rico a job. He became a fisherman. Lupe taught him how to set traps and he assisted with the fish market. Business was booming: it had gotten to the point where Lupe had to go fishing every day, twice a day. The mouth of the creek ran into the Gulf, which meant there was a constant supply.

Life on the Outback was good, and continued this way for years. Time flew by, Lupe was up in age and his steps were getting short. Mama Joyce's focus was on taking care of her husband. The fish market was totally in Rico's control.

Surprisingly, that wild Rico never returned. He remained a humble, hard worker and a great asset to Lupe and Mama Joyce. He was like the child that they never had.

Maddie, on the other hand, remained the same. She had a penchant for the wild side! She was now in love with another biker boy from the Hills and she worked at the local post office. She often went MIA on the weekends. Santiago finished high school and was now a freshman in college, 3 hours away.

The Lord had been dealing with Nate strongly about starting a church. Although he knew and recognized the voice of the Lord, Nate still had reservations.

"So what are you going to do, babe?" asked Silvia.

"I don't know; I know there's a need for a church here. Many people here are professing to have no religion; some are even atheist. The word of God needs to go forth, but how can I preach when I have such a wild child? My family is my first Ministry."

"I thought you told me that we were to do the fishing and God will do the washing? All we have to do is lead them to God: he will handle the rest. I'm 100% certain that pertains to your daughter, as well."

Nate stared at Sylvia in awe, considering how far God had bought her! The same woman he'd been teaching was now teaching him. "You are right, my love, I'm open to seeing how God's going to work this out!" Later that same evening, God sent confirmation, when Rico showed up at the house.

He found Nate and Silvia sitting on the porch. Addressing both of them as he approached, he asked to speak with Nate privately. The two of them took a walk.

"Mr. Nate, how do you know when God is talking to you? I've been reading my Bible. I don't understand a lot of it, but I do feel like God is talking to me. Trying to get my attention!"

"Wow!" replied Nate. "Well, God speaks in many ways. Sometimes it's in dreams, or it could be a quiet thought, something you feel deeply inside, also through other people, sometimes. Actually, he's been dealing with me. I told my wife today, I think God is leading me to start a church."

"Really, I'd come," said Rico eagerly.

"Well, I was wondering how to do it. God sent his answer through you. Bible study. I think we will start by having weekly Bible study at my house."

"Great sir, count me in," said Rico.

Nate was so anxious to get back into the house and tell Silvia the news. He found her on the phone with Santiago.

Thanksgiving was two weeks away. Santi was informing her that he would be bringing a guest. A female guest. Silvia was so excited!

Two days later, Lou called and said that he would be coming for Thanksgiving, as well. Not only would he be attending, but he would also be moving. He purchased a home in Richland, a few towns over. He would permanently be relocating to Australia! Nate was ecstatic!

"Well babe, seems like we will be having a house full, for Thanksgiving!"

"Yep, we better get prepared," said Silvia, smiling.

The Brodgen household was busy, as they prepared for the big day and their guests. Santiago and his guest arrived three days before Thanksgiving. The plan was to spend the three days before Thanksgiving with his family and the three days after Thanksgiving with her family. Unfortunately, things changed the moment he introduced her.

"Mom, Dad!" he yelled as he announced his arrival.

He found them in the kitchen. He gave them a hug and introduced his friend. "Mom and Dad, I'd like you to meet my girlfriend, Carmelita Venzino."

They both hugged and welcomed her to their home.

"Sweetie, what is your last name again?" Silvia asked.

"Venzino," replied Carmelita proudly.

Nate noticed Silvia's complexion became a shade lighter. For the first time in a long time, he saw fear in her eyes. He recognized it all too well. The same fear that he saw when she'd been chained to a bed years ago.

"Son, why don't you show Carmelita the grounds and take her to meet your grandma. She's been calling every two hours, to see if you'd arrived!"

"Sure, let's go, Carmelita." said Santi.

As soon as they left, Nate ran to his wife's side. He could tell that she was hanging on by a string. As soon as he touched her, she collapsed into his arms.

"Silvia, what is it? Please talk to me."

"Venzino, that's their last name! The people my dad sold me to! Oh God, and now my son is in love with one of them! Please, God, no! Nate, we can't! He can't! Our families cannot reconnect! The debt is not settled! Jesus! Jesus! I need to lay down!"

Nate escorted her to the bedroom. "I hate to do this, but baby, it's time. It's now or never; his life is in danger. It's time to tell him the whole truth! You lay here and relax. I'll handle this and return."

As Nate closed the bedroom door, he met Maddie in the hallway returning for one of her MIA sabbaticals. "Where have you been? Never mind—I'll deal with you later!

"Listen, your brother is here. He has brought home a lady-friend. I need to have a man-to-man talk with him for a minute. So I need you to keep her occupied for about 30 minutes. Can you do that for Daddy?"

"Daddy? Daddy, what's wrong?"

"Nothing, I just need 30 minutes alone with your brother. He's at Mama's. Call him, tell him that you're at home and you want to meet his lady-friend. We will meet them in the yard. You bring her in and give her a tour of the house, except for Mom's room. She's not feeling well."

"What's wrong with her? She was fine when I left!"

"Please, Maddie, work with me!" said Nate, in a slightly elevated tone.

"OK Dad, I got it. Calling him now," said Maddie.

Within a few minutes Santiago was in the yard, happy to see his big sister. He hugged Maddie and introduced her to Carmelita. On cue, Maddie chimed in with a bubbly spirit offering her a tour of the house. "I'll show you where you will be sleeping."

Nate quickly whisked his son away for the talk.

Sabrina Johnson Fye

"Dad, what's wrong—oh, I can see it in your face that something's not right."

"Everything is going to be fine, son. I just need to talk to you alone for a minute. How did you meet this girl? She seems nice."

"We met in the cafeteria at school. Her bestie dated my roommate."

"I see, do you know anything else about her? Her family, her upbringing?"

"Not really, I know of the area that she's from. That's why I'm going with her family for 3 days."

"I see," said Nate. "Son, I need to tell you something. Have a seat there, on that rock.

"You know that I was a military man, special ops, right? Well, I met your mother while I was on a mission. I told you that much, but we never told you guys the whole story."

So Nate began at the beginning, fighting back the tears as he spoke.

"Mercy! That's why Mom's skin is like that? I thought she had eczema or something." The news was more than Santiago could handle. Instead of sitting on the rock, he knelt over it and wailed.

"'So son, you see why we are worried! The debt hasn't been settled. Venzino is the last name of the man to whom your mom's family sold her. It's too dangerous for you to go there or continue to date this girl. Even the breakup has to be easy; these people are crazy!

"Yep, but first we have to prove that she's from

158

the same family. Even if she's not, your mom's kidnapping was the talk of the town; the whole area knew about it. Somebody's going to remember it and link you to it. We can't get involved with these people again."

"Trust me, after what they did to my mom, I don't want anything to do with any of them! I just want to kill him!"

"Wait, son, that's not the answer. It's over, your mom has healed and moved on. Let's just figure out how to get you out of this. Your mom's worried sick!"

"That's the key! I'll tell her I can't go because mom's sick. I'll drive her home, but I can't stay. I won't even get out of the car." "Sounds good," said Nate. "Meanwhile, I'll come up with a plan B just in case. As for now, son, you look like you've been crying. You need to pull yourself together and walk this out, at least until after Thanksgiving. We don't want to make her feel uncomfortable or suspicious. I know that's asking for a lot, but we have to do it, for Mom's sake!"

"Jesus, Dad, this is so hard! How can I face my mom without crying? Thanksgiving is going to be a disaster, and it's going to be my fault!"

"No, no it won't be a disaster. Son, you are a Brodgen. You're the spitting image of me, with a little Latino charm! You are physically and mentally strong! The son of a gladiator! You can do this! You have to, for your mother; she has suffered enough."

Santiago girded up his loins and continued their visit with no alarm to Carmelita. The day after

Thanksgiving, he told her the bad news that he wouldn't be going. However, as he drove her to the airport, his emotions ran rapidly. He wanted to see the guy that his mom was sold to. He only wanted a few minutes alone with him! This animal! Although he'd promised his dad that he wouldn't go, the more he tried to dismiss the thought, the stronger it got! Before he knew it, he'd boarded the plane alongside her. At this point, all he could do was pray.

Thanksgiving had been a little more than Silvia expected. She was emotionally, physically and spiritually exhausted. As she laid in bed with her husband, she suddenly had the urge to vomit. At that very moment, Nate received a text from Santiago: "Forgive me, Dad, I knowI promised I wouldn't go, but I can't fight this urge. I just want to see his face. I won't tell them who I am and I won't be in danger. I must go, I will be in touch!"

"Jesus!" yelled Nate, as he leapt to his feet. "No! No! No!"

"What?" asked Sylvia, running out of the bathroom.

Nate didn't have to answer, his face said it all.

"He went, didn't he?"

"He went, didn't he?" She repeated. "Please tell me, Nate, that he didn't go!"

Like a good soldier, Nate quietly stood at his post.

Silvia immediately fell to her knees in prayer. It was the only thing, the best thing that she could do for her son! Nate fell to his knees as well and prayed…

"Jesus! Lord, oh Merciful God, I beseech you on behalf of my child. I know what's going through his mind, but you said that vengeance is yours. I ask you to send a legion of angels to be encamped around him. Return him Lord without one hair on his head harmed. Amen."

Now feeling at peace, Silvia crawled back into bed and hugged her Bible as if it was a pillow. Nate got up and called Lou. He informed him of the situation and called for an emergency meeting.

"I thought we were trusting God," Silvia pointed out.

"Yes, baby, we are, but just in case he calls and says Dad I need you, I've got to be ready! I'm old now, this is not a one-man job. We asked God for a safe return. We don't know how he's going to do it. He sent me to get you a long time ago. This time, he could be sending me to get my son."

Silvia rolled over and began to pray in her Heavenly language. Nate met Lou at the door. The look on his face was indescribable. He loved Nate's children like his own. The two old friends embraced, trying to fight back the tears. "I told him not to go! I was sure that he heard me! He always listens!"

"He's a man now, a man wanting to defend his mother's honor. Not the wisest decision, but surely we both can understand that," said Lou.

"Now, I've been thinking. Hopefully we won't get the dreaded call, but if we do, time is of the essence. We have to be ready! No time to gather a crew, they need to be here! We need equipment on standby. I'm out too now, so that means I'll be calling for lots of favors.

"So what's the plan, since we both are out of the game?"

"Yes, so it's best to keep it that way. We need to play on our own field. I'm calling in renegades, retirees…and a couple of young bucks that opted out. They're old, but not dead! These skills are like second nature for us."

"OK, who do you have in mind?"

His thought was interrupted by the sound of gravel flying, as a car sped into the driveway. "I'll get it," said Lou, going to answer the door.

"Russell Scott a.k.a. 'The chameleon' reporting for duty, sir!" His eyes smarting, Nate got on his feet, saluted and then hugged his fellow soldier. Together they sat at the table, brainstorming. An hour later, a second car arrived; it was actually a van. The sound of laughter rang out from the yard. "Who's that, I wonder?" said Nate.

"Hang tight, they're coming in…" ordered Lou.

These men waited for no one to answer the door. They politely came into the house and marched in, saluting and introducing themselves.

"Levi Remington, a.k.a. 'Trigger', reporting for duty, sir!"

"Kash Washington, a.k.a. 'Bulletproof' reporting for duty, sir!"

"Dalton Oglesby, a.k.a. 'Santa Claus' reporting

for duty, sir!"

"Braxton Knight, a.k.a. 'Deuce' reporting for duty, sir!"

Nate stood at the table, quietly saluting. This time, he couldn't contain the tears that were rolling down his face. This kind of love could pierce a strong soldier's heart. He hadn't heard from or seen these fellas in years! A couple of them he'd never met, only heard of.

"Well, these are the best of the oldies," said Lou. "They put their families aside to come and take care of yours."

"Way down in the Outback, I must add," Kash chimed in, and they all laughed.

"Yes," laughed Nate. "Man, I thank you gentlemen. I thank all of you for coming. I will pay you—I'm not filthy rich but I can give each of you something!"

"It's not about the money. It's about brotherhood and the boy," said Dalton.

"As far as the money goes, his godfather has already taken care of it," added Lou.

"How did you get so much done in a few minutes? How did you get these guys here so fast?" asked Nate, still in amazement.

"Look, it's like this…m Charlie, you're the angels. I just know how to get a lot done in a few minutes!"

The guys laughed, trying to make light of the situation.

"Well, we're here and ready, so let's get a plan

together while we wait. Hopefully within a couple of hours, the boy will show up at the front door. However, just in case he calls … it's showtime!"

"So the bottom line is, whether he shows up or if we have to go in and get him, either way he's coming home!"

"Amen," they agreed, clapping.

Santiago sat quietly, staring out of the window most of the flight.

"Are you OK?" asked Carmelita. "You've been a little distant the whole holiday."

"No, not distant…just nervous, I guess. Before, I was nervous for you, now it's my turn."

"Don't worry, they are going to love you."

Yeah right, just like they loved the rest of my family, he thought to himself.

When the plane landed on a remote strip, Santiago's heart began to flutter!

"Wait, I thought this was a commercial flight?"

"Nope, we own our private airline, that's why we are on a jet, silly."

Santiago had been warring in his mind so much, he hadn't even noticed. One thing for sure, it was time to pull himself together! A stretch limo was waiting to carry them to their destination, the Venzino home. The limo pulled up to the gated mansion and Santiago's mouth dropped. It was massive!

"You didn't tell me that you were rich," he whispered to Carmelita.

"You never asked...why, does it matter?"

"Absolutely not," he replied.

Cars were in the driveway, which meant the family were awaiting their arrival. Before they could get out of the car, her mom appeared at the front door. Tears of joy in her eyes, they embraced. Santiago was totally disengaged. He could care less about meeting her parents. All he went to see was the face of the man that bought his mother. There were several older gentlemen there; Santiago was trying to figure out which one.

"Folks, this is my friend Santiago..."

The welcome was fairly dry and cold. Only a few of the elderly women tried to make him feel welcome.

Santiago's heart broke at the sight of an elderly maid almost tripping trying to carry a tray of hors d'oeuvres to the guests. His first instinct was to run to help her. As he started to walk in her direction, Carmelita grabbed his arm and shook her head no.

When the old woman approached him, she looked up in his face and involuntarily dropped the tray.

"Old lady!" yelled a man from across the room. He had to be Carmelita's father.

"I don't know why you don't just fire her! She's too old to work," said Carmen.

"Only when her toes are pinned together," replied the man.

Wow, this was a new and disgusting side of Carmen Santiago had never seen before.

Everyone moved to the formal dining room for

dinner. It seemed as if the dining room table seated 30 people. It was the longest table Santiago had ever seen! Thanksgiving in this house was a sumptuous feast. The maids and servers were constantly making trips back and forth from the kitchen to bring out food. The table was laden

Santiago had an eerie feeling, as if someone were watching him. He tried to be fake by smiling and observing at the same time. Suddenly his eyes met those of the elderly maid. The little old woman was standing at the entrance of the kitchen, staring into the dining room at him. He politely nodded and smiled. She quickly turned and went back into the kitchen.

Then she returned carrying a large gravy boat and some rolls. She began serving the people at the far end of the table and working her way towards him. By the time she reached Santiago, her arms were tired and her hands trembling. She tripped and spilled gravy down the front of his shirt.

"OMG Daddy! Please, get rid of her! She's too old, look how she's ruined his shirt!" yelled Carmelita.

"I'm so sorry mister, I apologize. Come, I will clean you up right away. I will give you one of Mr. Antonio's shirts."

Riddled with confusion and disgust, he followed the old woman into the kitchen. Suddenly, she grabbed his hand and dragged him into the laundry room.

"Mister, I am sorry! Well, actually, I'm not. I must ask you, what is your mother's name?"

CHAPTER EIGHT

Before he could say anything, she answered her own question.

"Mister, is your mother's name Silvia?" Santiago could see the tears in her eyes.

"Yes ma'am," he said.

"Jesus Lord...I knew it, when I saw you! I knew that you were hers."

The news was so overwhelming it brought her to her knees.

"Hijo (son), I am your abuela (grandma)."

"I knew it was you! There is a God! You are the spitting image of my Silvia! When she escaped, they came back, killed her father and now I'm paying for the rest of the debt. I won't be here many years more. I can't let the sins of your grandfather fall on you. I won't!"

Santiago immediately transitioned into using Spanish, which he didn't often do.

"They don't know who I am," said Santiago.

"Oh, but they will. By tonight they will, I promise you! Hurry, change into this shirt while I change into my sneakers."

"Wait, abuela! What are you doing?"

"I'm getting you out of here! Quick, grab my bag," she said, pointing to the backpack in the corner. "I'm gonna leave these right here!" She left her maid shoes on the top of the dryer.

"I don't know if this is a good idea, abuela, you can't run!"

"Please, hijo…come on, trust me!" Santiago grabbed the bag as ordered and followed her out the back door. His heart was racing, 5 miles a minute.

Abuela quietly crept down the side of the house and pressed her weight against the concrete fence. The wall moved and the door opened. "This is one of their emergency escape routes," she whispered. "The exit will lead us to the river." She was tiptoeing so slowly; Santiago knew that they were bound to get caught. She must have arthritis or something, he thought. Surely, by now someone knew that they were missing! The story of his mom's rescue popped into his mind. He remembered his dad telling him how he carried her out.

"Wait, wait a minute, Abuela…" He quickly swung the book bag around, strapping it on to his chest. Then, he knelt down in front of her. "Come on, abuela, get on my back."

"Oh no, hijo, I'm too heavy!" Santiago had to fight back, his smile. "Grandma, look at me. I'm a big boy! I play football! I promise you, I won't drop you. We must go!"

With a little assistance from Santiago, she hopped onto his back like a little child.

"OK abuela, hold onto the backpack straps in front of me! Hold tight!"

"Si hijo...go!" she said.

As she held on, Santiago jogged towards the exit. He thanked God there was just enough light to see where he was going. As she promised, the exit led to the river.

"Now what, abuela? Put me down and get the rowboat over there," she ordered.

"Grandma I can't put you in the water. We don't have life jackets and the water is a little swift." "I'll be fine soon, come on and put these muscles to work."

Again, Santiago did as ordered. He really didn't think that it was a good idea; but there was no turning back! While he rowed, she fished around in her bag.

"What are you looking for?"

"My flashlight. The river will lead us to the back of the jungle, but we will be OK."

"What? The jungle? Jeez, grandma, there are snakes in there!"

"They're also snakes on our trail. I guess we have to decide which ones we'd rather face!"

With one last stroke, the boat hit the bank. The old lady reached under her dress.

Santiago closed his eyes. "Open your eyes, hijo...let's go," she said, laughing while rolling down the legs of her jeggings.

Santiago laughed, "You had on pants?"

"Yes, this is also why I gave you a long sleeve shirt. The jungle can be cold at night. Now let's go—I know where a cave is, not far from here."

Jungles, cave, snakes, it was all quite a lot for Santiago. He picked a big stick to use as a staff. With his elderly grandma on his back, he proceeded.

She held the flashlight as he weaved through the jungle. Ironically, it seemed as if her hands didn't have the trembles anymore.

"Ooh, hijo, careful— big snake on your left," she directed.

Santiago jumped so hard, he almost lost her!

"Easy, big boy, calm down and keep moving...that one isn't poisonous."

"Jesus help me!" cried Santiago.

God answered his prayer. Within minutes, they'd reached the mountainside.

"OK, what now, grandma?"

"OK, we have two choices...either we elevate, or hide in plain sight."

"Elevate—you mean rock climbing? It's dark and we only have one flashlight. Besides, who takes their elderly grandma rock climbing? No, no ma'am...hiding in plain sight it is!"

"I can do it son, it's only a few feet up. We must elevate, this area will be swarming soon! I was born an athlete, a rock climber! I climbed even when I was pregnant!"

Santiago pleaded with her not to.

"OK scaredy pants, I know of another place where we can hide. It's going to be about another mile."

"That's fine, I'll carry you. Hop back on, he said. I'll even carry you two more miles, but I will not let my abuela climb a mountain!"

"Eighty-three," she said, repositioning herself on his back. I'm eighty-three years old, just in case you were wondering." Then, she rubbed his curly hair.

"You know what, my mom does that. I guess now I'll have two of you making me feel like a four-year-old again."

"Yes, you will. Now let's hurry, son. We will have to cut off the flashlight soon."

She was right; the walk was about another mile. The jungle had thinned out into mostly shrubbery. "Turn here and put me down, son," she directed.

Santiago turned and put her down.

She led him between two cleft rocks. It was so tight, Santiago could barely squeeze in. There at the back was a little duck-in hole. It wasn't big enough to call it a cave. She took his stick and beat the ground and the roof, checking for bats and snakes.

"Well, it looks like it's vacant! Can I have my bag please?"

Santiago gave it to her. Apparently, she knew what she was doing—she took out a tablecloth and laid it on the ground. "This will keep us off the cold jungle floor. It's not much, but they'll keep the ants away." Then she pulled out a sheet, four bottles of water and some glow sticks.

"Grandma, let me quickly contact my dad. I know they're waiting to hear from me."

Santiago thought about using his special phone that his godfather had given him on graduation day. Then, he remembered that Lou had retired. He took out his cell phone, but had no bars of service. "OMG, what am I going to do?"

"Do you want to use mine?"

"You have a cell phone, abuela?"

"Si (yes)."

She reached into her apron pocket and pulled out a little flip phone, with large letters and numbers. It was a Jitterbug.

Instead of calling, Santiago texted in Morse code. His dad taught it to him as a little boy. His first text was "Godfather, S.O.S."

At this point, back at his family home, the guests were spread all throughout Nate's house.

"Nate!" yelled Lou, jumping to his feet.

The way that he said his name, everyone knew that it had to be Santiago. The cavalry came running into the den.

"Nate, he says help!"

"Where are you and are you okay?" Lou texted back.

"Yes, I'm fine. Escaped with my abuela. Mom's mom. Please hurry and track this phone. My cell is dead!" was Santiago's response.

"Got it, hold tight! Don't move, we will be there soon!"

"They are looking for us, Godfather. Abuela had to pay after Mom escaped. They took out Grandpa!

"Coordinates are locked in. Dad says good job, and whatever you do…don't move!

OTW…Go ahead, you know what to do!"

"They're coming, abuela! Sorry, but I must kill your phone." He took his staff and smashed the phone into pieces. Just as Santiago settled in beside her, it began to rain, and his stomach growled.

"I knew that you would be hungry," she said.

She reached into her backpack and pulled out a gallon-size bag of cheese, crackers and other hors d'oeuvres.

"What! Really?" said Santiago, laughing.

"Oh wait, there's more." She then pulled out a bag of black cherries and chicken wings.

Santiago laughed until tears were in his eyes.

"Abuela, I don't understand how you did all this so quickly, without anyone noticing. I mean, you barely tip around!"

"I know how to tip fast when I need to," she laughed. "You see, living this kind of lifestyle keeps you in survival mode. You have to think fast on your feet and be ready to run, at all times. The moment you walked through the door, I knew that you were mine. You look just like my Silvia. I went to my room, grabbed my bag and hid it in the washroom. The holidays are a big performance for the Venzino family. Everyone must be working at 100%. Plus, they give a bonus for good service on the holidays."

"Well, I guess you lost yours," said Santiago, laughing.

"Forget about it! All I knew was that I had to get you out of there! So I went to the kitchen while it was empty and I loaded up on food. Packed my backpack, then I proceeded to smother you in gravy and now here we are!"

"What about the glow sticks?"

"The kids have them left over, from birthday parties every year. I keep a few in my bag and in my drawer in case the lights go out. An old lady needs to be able to see," she laughed.

The rain was pouring, the temperature was dropping, and Santiago could tell she was getting cold. She had on her maid's sweater, but it wasn't warm enough.

"Oh, and I almost forgot. Here, one for me and one for you." She pulled two little snug caps out of her pocket.

"Abuela—did you leave the kitchen sink?" he asked.

"I think so," she laughed.

Santiago quickly finished eating enough to satisfy his hunger. He knew that the food had to last until help arrived. Abuela packed the food back into the bag and zipped it up.

"I'm going to put this big stick here at the entrance. That way, nothing can cross it without me hearing." He leaned back against the mountain wall and beckoned for his abuela to come close. "Lean on me, abuela, and rest. Help will be here soon." Santiago could tell that she was freezing by the way that she was shaking. He had to do something to keep her warm. Lighting a fire was out of the question; it would be a dead giveaway to their location.

He opened his legs and gestured to her to come. "Come sit here, abuela, and let me help to keep you warm." "No that's okay, you don't have to do that," she declined.

"Yes, I do, I can't let you freeze." Santiago patted the ground with his hand, giving in as his grandma came over and sat down. He took the sheet and wrapped it around them both. He only hoped his body was enough to keep her warm. They heard voices and footsteps all through the night. "Don't worry hijo, no one will ever think to squeeze between those rocks, she whispered." Santiago rubbed his abuela's arms as she held onto the sheet. He sat there and prayed.

Dear God, please keep us safe and warm. I can't wait to see the look on my mom's face when she sees her. Please let Dad get here soon. Hide us from the enemy, Lord I pray...Amen.

His abuela was now shaking so hard, her teeth were chattering. She could barely keep her mouth closed. Obviously, this wasn't working, she needed more heat.

"OK, abuela, this isn't working; we need to try something else. Let's try this, OK? I need you to lay down along the wall. I'm going to get close and hover over you. I promise not to squeeze you." They shuffled around in the dark in the little den, underneath the rock.

"OK," abuela agreed. Tucked in close, Santiago used his body to block the jungle draft from her.

"Better?" he asked.

"Much better," she confirmed. "Thanks."

Nate and his crew moved in slowly and carefully. The plan was to avoid altercation by any means necessary. They weren't young men anymore. All they wanted was the boy and the old lady. By daylight the rain had ceased and left a light fog over the jungle.

Nate followed the transmitter's signal deeper into the jungle towards the clearance.

"We're getting close," Nate said to Kash. He was the youngest of the group and chose to go with Nate, while the others trailed behind covering from a distance.

Around noon, the fog had completely lifted. "OK fellas, everyone keep your eyes peeled and your ears open. The fog has lifted, and our camouflage is gone. At any moment we could be sitting ducks," said Nate into the radio.

To keep the cartel from tracking their radio signal, they replied by saluting one by one, instead of responding. With their eyes on the prize, they kept moving.

Santiago and his abuela made it through the night. He was awakened by her tapping on his chest.

"Oh, come on, Big Boy, wake up!" Like all grandmas the first thing she wanted to do was feed him. "Well, looks like we made it," she said as she went through her bag, getting food and water. "Oh, I forgot

I had this," she added, pulling out a butcher knife and handing it to him.

"Ha, easy with that thing, lady," he laughed with his hands up in surrender. "Thanks!" He carefully took it out of her little wrinkled hand.

They whispered and laughed as they ate their brunch. Time was moving on and the sun was warming up their den. "Hijo, I hate to worry you with this, but I'm an old lady and I need to pee," said his grandma.

He didn't know what to do. Nate had specifically said, don't move. He knew his dad was tracking with a weak signal, it was hot, and now his abuela needed to pee. He had to decide!

"OK abuela, just step outside the entrance to the side. I'm right here with the knife, but don't squeeze between the rocks". With his back turned, he sat on guard waiting for her to finish.

It was amazing how fast he was forming a bond with this old lady. She was tugging on his heart strings. It was like he'd known her all his life. He would do anything to protect her. They sat with their backs against the rock, trying to keep as cool as possible. The temperature continued to rise.

"Abuela, tell me about my mother, how she was as a little girl."

"Oh, my Silvia, she was something else." Hot and exhausted as she was, she whispered story after story, trying to keep their minds off their situation. In a couple of hours, the sun would be down. Santiago began to worry.

Where are they? Dad should have been here by now. God, I hope that they didn't catch them. I pray that they don't catch us! He didn't know how much more his abuela could take! The heat was taking a toll on her and she only had two bottles of water left.

"Maybe we should stop talking for a while, let's just save our energy," Santiago suggested. "Stop worrying, hijo, we will be okay, just pray," she whispered.

Did she just say pray? he thought to himself. He thought his mom said that she was raised to be an atheist. Well, it seems as if at some point, Grandma had an encounter with the Lord. He couldn't wait to hear this story. Due to the circumstances, it would have to wait.

"We're close," said Nate to Kash, looking at his watch.

"You said that an hour ago," he replied.

"I don't know what's happening, this signal is glitching in and out."

"Well, all I know is we have circled this area three times. We're tired and exhausted, we can't keep doing this."

"OK let's go back up here a little piece, I saw a spot under the trees to camp and take a break," said Nate.

Just as they were passing a big rock, he heard a sneeze.

"Bless you," said Nate

"What? I didn't sneeze," Kash replied.

The jungle draft made Santiago's sinuses flare up. So tired, hot and fatigued was he, he didn't even realize that he was sneezing so loudly.

"Ahh choo! Ahh choo! Ahh choo!"

"Nate, stop! It sounds like it's coming from the crack between those rocks. Surely no one would try to squeeze between them? There's no telling what's living back there," said Kash.

Confirmation came as he was trying to dismiss the thought.

"Ahh choo!"

"Somebody's definitely in there," said Kash, throwing his backpack and gear to the ground.

Nate did the same. "Wait, let me go for a first date," he insisted.

He switched on the micro flashlight attached to his gun and squeezed through. In the back of the den, he could see the silhouette of two bodies.

"Santiago," he said in a low tone. "Santiago, are you in there? Santiago, is that you?" Hot, drained and almost delirious, Santiago opened his eyes, long enough to see the silhouette of a man. It looked like his dad, but he wasn't sure. Nate called him one more time. "Santiago?"

"Dad, is that you?"

"Yes, son, hold on—we're coming in to get you!"

Kash patiently waited outside as the other members held the post clear. Nate quickly squeezed back out, sweat pouring down his face. "It's him in there! But we got to hurry, it's got to be a hundred and ten degrees in there."

"OK, let me go, I'm smaller," said Kash.

"Here, take this, and I'll keep you drag them out."

He handed him the parachute carrier that he had used with Silvia years ago. It was still in perfect condition.

"Kash, introduce yourself. He has a knife. We don't want him to think that you're the enemy."

"Will do, boss!"

Kash wormed through the crack, dropped to his knees and crawled to the edge of the den.

"Santiago, my name is Kash," he began. "I'm a part of your dad's crew. We came to get you."

"No—take my abuela first."

"OK, I'm coming in," said Kash.

The moment he hit the lair he agreed with Nate: the air was stifling! It was amazing that they were still alive. He quickly rolled the old lady onto the carrier. Jesus, he said as he rolled her over. She was in bad shape. Moving as quickly as he could, he dragged her back through the crack. Then he threw the straps to Nate. Nate pulled as hard as he could. Her frail body maneuvered quickly through the rocks.

"Ha, man, somebody get Deuce now, she needs help ASAP." Nate signaled and Dalton and Deuce quickly moved in while the remaining two held post.

"My God," said Deuce. Dalton quickly swept the little old lady up into his arms and carried her to the canopy of trees.

"My son," said Nate.

"On my way back, boss," said Kash as he pulled the parachute back into the lair. To his surprise, Santiago had mustered up enough energy to drag himself to the entrance, and then passed out.

Kash's heart began to pound profusely! God, please don't let him be dead. I cannot deliver him to his father this way!

He rolled Santiago's almost lifeless body onto the carrier. He struggled through the crack, backing himself out, pulling Santiago behind him. Once they were out Nate took over and quickly pulled his son out into the opening.

When he saw him and his condition he panicked!

"Santiago, can you hear me? It's Daddy! I'm here! I'm here, son!" Nate smacked his hand just like he did his mother's years ago.

Russell took over. OK Nate, give him some room. We got him, he needs Deuce's help. They picked the big guy up by the hands and feet and carried him over to Deuce. He was still working with his grandmother.

The guys quickly moved Santiago in and laid him beside her. Deuce was hanging her IV on a limb in the tree. Nate helplessly gazed at his son and mother-in-law. He couldn't believe he was going through this again.

Deuce gave Dalton the eye, to look at Nate. He in turn signaled for Levi to come take him away.

"Let's get you some water and a little rest," said Levi, escorting him to the other side of the tree.

"I'm okay, just never thought I'd have that feeling again. That feeling of helplessness, there's nothing that I can do."

"You can pray. Then we can go over the strategy, how we're going to get out of here. You've already done the hard part, you found them! Now let God and Deuce handle the rest. The boy is going to be fine. He's a junior Gladiator. Hasn't he proven that?"

"Yes, he has. If the old lady's anything like Silvia, she's quite a pistol herself!"

"Exactly, now let's get a quick prayer in and figure out what to do."

As soon as they finished praying, Russell and Kash joined them. "Ha, me and Kash are going to scout the place out a little bit. We have to move them before it gets dark. They've already been exposed to being overheated. We don't want to shock them by getting too cold tonight," said Russell.

"Yeah it's quite a few of us; we best not waste time. Things seem to be dry right now. I don't think anybody's in the area looking for them, but we can't guarantee that it's going to stay that way."

"Are you sure that you don't need a little more rest?" asked Levi.

"Nope, we'll leave that for the old folks! We need to find some shelter. We all have families to get back home to."

"Amen. If you need us, you know what to do."

With the jungle at their back the two guys moved through the green shrubbery. They walked for about

10 minutes, then stopped in their tracks.

"Well, look at God!" Russell exclaimed.

Right around the bend on the other side of the den was a huge cave.

"Wow. That looks like a big, deep cave. We should probably get a little backup when we're going in there." Not saying anything, Kash clicked his radio receiver three times; within minutes, Nate and Levi came striding through the shrubs.

"We're good," said Russell, "but look what we found." He pointed up towards the big cave. "We need to check it out!"

"OK, let's move in." With guns drawn and adrenaline pumping, the guys searched the cave and found it empty.

"We'll go back for the others. You guys collect firewood and bedding," said Nate.

While collecting firewood, Russell reached down to pick up a stick—and it moved.

"OMG, Kash! Kash, come here, quick!"

As he approached, Russell yelled, "Now stop!"

"Bro, I'm standing right here on a bed of boas!"

"Constrictors?"

"Yes!"

"Four of them are here, by my left foot. I can't move!"

Kash aimed his gun.

"Dude, watch the foot, please...I need it," Russell pleaded.

"Chill out man, I wasn't awarded top sniper in my

division for nothing! Now, hold still!"

Seconds later, the job was complete. "Well, looks like we got lucky! We got wood, bedding and supper. I'm tired of that ration anyway !" Everyone laughed.

Nate and the crew arrived to a welcoming sight. The fellows laid banana and palm leaves on the floor for bedding and their food was on the fire. Santiago seemed to be coming around, but the old lady was still in critical condition. They laid both of them on the leaves.

"How are they looking?" asked Kash.

"I've given both of them two bags of IV. I only have two more left. I'm hoping that they will come around soon. They were roasting in that den. I can't believe that they stayed there," said Russell.

"Well, that's partly my fault. I told him that whatever he did, he shouldn't move. For once he listened to me...unfortunately."

"Don't be hard on yourself, man, if he hadn't listened, it's most likely they would have been captured," said Dalton.

The guys feasted on boas and water, then scheduled the watch.

Nate and Braxton took first watch.

During the middle of the night, the old lady woke up screaming at the top of her lungs. All that she knew was that she was in a different place and surrounded by men! Her cry awakened Santiago.

"Abuela, abuela, calm down!"

Out of nowhere, he became his mom's son. His

Spanish kicked in and he began to pour into his grandma. The only thing Nate understood was "mi padre"...my father.

His mom would have been proud!

"Abuela, this is your son-in-law Nathaniel," said Santiago, introducing his father.

Her tears of fear immediately turned into tears of joy!

"Abuela, he rescued your Silvia and now he's here to rescue us."

"Thank you, thank you, thank you," she cried. "I prayed and I knew that my daughter was somewhere safe."

"Well she wasn't, but she is now," Nate reassured her.

"I knew this boy was my grandson the moment that he walked through the door. I could see my Silvia in him. So I immediately started preparing to get him out of there! He will not pay for the sins of his grandfather!"

"I can't believe that you guys stayed in that hot little den," Braxton put in.

"Only because my hijo was too chicken to let me climb the rocks. I know of some good hiding places up a little bit higher. But he wouldn't let me climb!"

"How old are you, ma'am?" Levi asked.

"Eighty-three," she responded proudly.

"Exactly. Who takes their eighty-three year old grandma mountain climbing?" said Santiago, laughing.

"Oh, I could do it!" she snapped.

"I know, I believe you, ma'am!" Nate interrupted, seeing that she was getting upset.

I think everyone should lie back down and rest. Wwe have a long hike out of here tomorrow."

As they settled down Nate texted Lou.

"Charlie, you have another angel."

It had been hours since they'd found them. He couldn't believe that he'd forgotten to update Silvia.

"Great, Santa's sleigh is ready," Lou responded.

"OK, but Santa says he's bringing an extra present."

"Affirmative."

"Ha! Everybody, Nate just texted they have the boy!"

So relieved from fear, Silvia passed out at the good news. Only this time, Nate was not there to catch her.

"Mama!" Maddie screamed as she hit the floor. Everyone ran to her aid. Within minutes, she was fully alert again.

"Thank you Jesus, thank you Jesus," she cried. She couldn't wait until her family was back together again.

A little before dawn Nate and Braxton switched places with Levi and Russell. They let Dalton get a full night's sleep because he was Santa. It was his job to fly them out. They wanted to make sure that he was well rested. They shared the rest of the snake, ration and water. When the fog lifted, they were ready to move out.

"Abuela, ma'am... you might want to strip down to your T-shirt and your leggings," Nate suggested.

"What? Why?"

"Because it's hot and Kash and Braxton will be taking turns carrying you."

"Oh no, I'm fine—I can walk!"

"Yes, I know you can, ma'am. I know that you can handle it! But we don't know the layout of the area, like you do. I was thinking that we could use the extra set of eyes."

"Nope, I can walk and see at the same time," she snapped.

Nate should have known that reverse psychology would not work on this old lady.

"I'll carry her," Santiago interrupted.

"Are you sure, son? Do you feel strong enough?"

"Yes Dad, I'm fine, plus she doesn't know them."

"Well, since you need my help, I'll keep my eyes open, if my hijo carries me," pronounced abuela.

"Great, then it's settled. Thank you, ma'am, for being such a team player. I see that you're going to fit right in.

Jeez, another Silvia, Nate thought, smiling.

Abuela did as agreed. Santiago helped her into the carrier and the guys strapped her on.

"OK fellas, let's move fast and keep it tight! Keep your eyes and ears open! Remember that we are carrying precious cargo," Nate briefed.

As soon as Santiago took his first step, his abuela leaned in and planted a little kiss on his cheek. "Come on, Big Moses, get me out of here. Take me home, to your mama." With those words alone, she melted the hearts of six men. Santiago instantly gained the strength of ten gladiators. Now he too was on a mission! Ever since that day, she called him "Big Moses". They hiked for hours with no interference.

"I'm surprised it's so dry? Surely they haven't given up this easily," mused Russell.

"I don't know…something definitely doesn't feel right."

Finally, they reached the ocean. Lou had pulled a few strings and had a seaplane waiting.

"No sign of heat, something definitely is off. They have to be up to something," said Levi.

The guys helped abuela into the boat, then the plane. Once again, Santiago's legs were on fire but he would never tell anyone. Today he wasn't Nate's son, he was a soldier!

From that point on, Dalton took over. He texted Lou, "Santa's on his way with a full bag of presents." Lou was sitting on the porch when he got the news.

"They are airborne!" he yelled, bursting through the door. "They're on their way home!"

This time, Mama Joyce wept with tears of joy. All of Nate's missions were private. Now she was glad that they were; her heart couldn't take it!

The smooth ride put abuela to sleep. She woke up in a panic, yelling "Hijo, hijo, can you hear me?

"Yes, ma'am," he answered, "but I could hear you better if you didn't yell."

"Hijo, did you drink anything at the house?"

"Yes ma'am, I had a glass of champagne and some soda."

"Oh my, my, my," she responded, before turning to her native language.

"Really, Abuela? "Is that what you think is happening?"

The rest of the gang patiently waited for these two to translate what they thought was going down.

"Nathaniel, it's my hijo—he used a glass; they're now running his prints. That's what they do. Sometimes, instead of hunting them down they go straight to them!"

"What, that means they could be sitting in my yard, when we get there!"

"Not necessarily so. You guys live off the grid, remember. There's probably no prints in the system ."

"Yeah, but I brought her home to our family. I brought the enemy straight to our front door!" "It's OK, son, you didn't know. Don't worry, everything is going to be alright," said Nate.

Abuela took Santiago's hand in her small hand and held it. The two had definitely created a bond in just a few short hours.

"Don't worry, son, I would die before I let them take you," she said.

"Whoa…wait a minute, nobody's dying! We're all going home and we're going to be just fine! God has gotten us all out safely. He's not going to leave us now! We will be OK, trust me—better yet, trust God!" Nate testified.

"Dalton, what is the time looking like?" "We'll be landing in 4 hours 36 seconds, sir," he responded.

"Great, I guess I need to call Lou."

"Ha, how are you guys?" he asked, answering.

"Tired but fine. I wanted to update you." Then, he informed him of the whole situation.

"Wow, so I need to beef up security! Honestly Nate, I don't have any other retirees that I trust. You've got the whole crew. I know, so do me a favor. Tell Dhunganda the situation. Ask him to see if he can pull some of his warrior friends from the hills. Tell them it's not a favor, but it's a job. I'm paying!"

"I'm sure you can handle the rest. I'm not worried. We will see you in a few hours."

"Will do, see you soon, Sabrina."

"Who?"

"You know I'm Charlie...you are Sabrina, one of my angels."

"Really, not now bro, not now!" he hung up, laughing.

Time passed quickly. Before they knew it, they were at a private airport 35 miles out of their hometown.

"I can't thank you enough for coming and doing this for me," Nate said gratefully, close to tears. "You gave me back my child."

"Didn't your mom tell you that big boys don't cry?" teased Russell, lightening the serious moment.

They all laughed. "We aren't leaving you just yet.

We've discussed it and decided to stick around, for two more days. If everything is still cool then we will go home," said Braxton.

They pulled up to the farm to find people buzzing around as if they were preparing for World War III. The women made sure each house was stocked with food. Dhunganda and Rico made sure each house had a good supply of firewood. Lupe tested all the generators, while Rod took care of the warriors. The hill warriors set up tents to the back of Arkarma's house.

"Dude, it looks like you don't need us," said Levi.

"Oh, indeed I do, you are professionals," Nate replied.

Silvia had no idea that her mom was coming. As the SUV pulled into the yard, she came running out to meet her family. Nate immediately jumped out and closed his door. Santiago and the other guys followed suit.

Silvia shouted, "Santiago!" who ran to pick her up. He planted kisses all over her face while she smacked him on the side of his head, playfully.

"OK, I deserve that and I'm sorry! I'm sorry that I lied; but I'm not sorry that I went. I bought you a little something back," he told her.

"What is it?" she asked.

Nate opened the passenger door and there sat her mother, in tears.

"Jesus, Mama! Mama, is that you?"

"Si, hija(daughter)!" Silvia fell to her knees and

wept. She cried for all those years that she thought she'd never see her mother again. She cried because she thought that she might never hold her baby boy once again. Reunions were more than any of them could take. True love will make gladiators, snipers, pilots, medics and warriors cry. Even the driver was in tears.

"My love, what happened? What happened to your face, your skin?" her mom questioned.

"Come on in. Mama, rest and I will tell you all about it later."

"Come on guys, and shower up and eat. We have food prepared for you. Some of you can shower at our house," Mama Joyce directed. One by one, they showered and entered the kitchen to eat. The women had food for days. "Man, look at the food," said Kash.

"Don't be shy, boys, come on, eat up, you deserve it," said Lupe.

"I don't know, on second thought, for this kind of treatment I might need to relocate to the Outback. I'm a single man," raved Braxton.

"Come on, move down here, we will find a good woman for you," Arkarma chimed in, laughing.

Silvia was grateful that Nate took her advice when remodeling the cottage to an open floor plan. Now he could actually see how great it worked. The kitchen and living room were full. People were sitting at the table, the island, sofas and even the floor all fellowshipping, loving, laughing and thanking God for the victory.

"Well, I feel that there is a need to make a speech," said Santiago, standing. "First of all, I want to say sorry to my parents for what I put them through. Thank you, to my brave abuela, for getting me out of there! To you guys, my father and my godfather, I thank you for coming to my rescue. I thank God we're all safe, and I pray it will remain that way!"

"Good job, son. You're welcome, we love you," said Lou, hugging his godson.

"Now if you guys are finished, we have other hungry warriors to feed," said Lupe.

The women began to fix plates and sent them to the guys on duty outside.

They were on high alert.

Day one went by with no sign of the cartel. On day two, just as they were preparing for supper, one of the warriors radioed in, "Code Blue!" Three black SUVs were coming down the main road towards the house.

Everyone scrambled, taking their positions. Nate moved his family into the barn at the back of the house.

"OK guys, stay put. Silvia, you've got your pink pearl; if anyone comes through those doors that you don't recognize, use it!"

"Si, Papi."

"I love all of you. Don't worry, this will be over soon."

Silvia said a quick prayer of protection over her family and friends, as he returned to the others. Nate ran back and joined Kash on the front porch.

He already briefed his people not to fire unless necessary. He was trying to end it as peacefully as possible. Three guys got out of the SUVs and approached Nate.

"I think that is far enough gentlemen, you can stop right there," Nate commanded. "I'm pretty sure that you saw the 'No Trespassing' sign and the sign that said 'Private Property'!"

"No comprende," said one of them sarcastically.

An elderly man stepped out in front. "Mister, I am…"

"I know exactly who you are," Nate interrupted.

"Good. If you know who I am, then you also know why we are here. You have something that belongs to me."

"Like what?" inquired Nate.

"My property!" the man spat.

"Property? Excuse me, but what property?"

"Don't play games with me! Either you can give it back, or I will take it back! Maybe even with a little interest, do you know what I mean? Either way, we're not leaving here empty-handed!"

"No, my friend, you'll be lucky to leave here with a limp. I really would like to end this peacefully," said Nate.

"Don't you think I know about your measly four-man crew?

"Measly?" Kash chimed in.

"Watch this…he snapped his finger; six armed men jumped out of each SUV.

Nate laughed. "Really. Now if you think that was something, then watch this!" He stuck his fingers in his mouth and whistled.

Aborigine warriors surrounded them. They jumped out of trees, fox dens, off the roof, everywhere! With their weapons drawn and war paint on…they came to declare war!

Some had guns, others had bows and arrows; either way the message was clear, that they meant business.

"I told you this is private property," Nate growled. "Do you believe me now?"

Nate gave the guys a signal to stand down, but they ignored it. They stood there, weapons drawn, waiting for someone to make a move.

"Impressive, very impressive…" said the old man, clapping his hands. "That still doesn't cover the fact that you owe me. I want my property back! Even if you kill us all, the debt is still unsettled. It will never be settled until I say so! I mean, do you know who I am?"

"No. The question is, do you know who I am? This family has suffered enough! That old debt has been paid in full and this is stopping TODAY!"

"Says who?"

"Says me!"

"Again, who are you?"

Nate stepped forward and whispered. The man looked as if he'd seen a ghost!

"Yes! Now like I said, this ends today! With one phone call, I can literally create World War III!" The men took a step back, with their hands in surrender!

"No, no! You're not going anywhere; not until this is finished!" Nate demanded. "I want to hear you say it. Confess it: the Castillo debt is paid in full!"

The guys began to speak.

"No, no," said Nate. "I want the old man to confess it!" The leader said it, reluctantly.

"No, say it loud! Don't go girlie on us now! Say it so all of us can hear it!" Levi yelled from the roof.

"The Castillo debt is paid in full!" the old man yelled.

"Now, that's more like it!" Levi replied.

"As of today, this is done! No more! Now get your measly men and get off my property!" ordered Nate.

The men got into their trucks, but the Aborigines did not budge. They stood their ground, weapons drawn. Nate chuckled, then walked up to the passenger window of the elderly man's vehicle.

"Now you know...if you say 'excuse me' nicely, they just might let you go."

The driver unfastened his seatbelt to get out, but Nate stopped him.

"No, no, not you...him," he said, gesturing towards the leader.

The leader smacked the dashboard in fury. Then, he took his seat belt off and got out again. He stood in the door and turned around.

"Excuse me, gentlemen. Do you mind letting us go?"

On cue, the men parted, and the trucks backed

out, exiting the property.

All the people cheered and laughed.

"Who's measly now?" laughed Levi.

"I wonder what he told them," said Lupe.

"He told them who he is. Who he really is. It's the first time he's ever owned up to it," said Mama Joyce.

Nate ran to get his family, announcing himself at the door. He remembered that his wife was "trigger happy" and a direct shot! Santiago opened the door.

"It's done! It's over and they're gone!" Nate told them.

"What do you mean, it's finished?" asked Silvia in disbelief.

"The debt has been paid in full. He just announced it to the world!"

"Really?" asked abuela.

"Dad, what did you do?"

"Let's just say I handled it, son. These enemies won't be bothering us again...ever! From this day forward, we will not even speak the Venzino name! Now come on, we're celebrating! Oh, but I wish that you could have seen it. The warriors had them surrounded!"

Nate filled them in on all the excitement they missed! He didn't leave out one detail. As the family walked around the house, the whole front yard cheered!

Now that the debt was settled, it was safe for Nate to say thank you and goodbye to his comrades.

He thanked his aborigine friends and paid each of them $200.00 for the two days of service. Although they'd done it free of charge, he and Lou went half and half depositing $3,000 in each team member's bank account. You couldn't put a price on life, but Nate wanted to show them a token of his appreciation.

They all were grateful to be returning to normal life. That night in bed, Lupe had questions.

"You never told me who Nate said that he was," Lupe said to Mama Joyce.

"That's because until today he's never acknowledged it. Let's just say I know where my granddaughter gets her attraction to bad boys. My son...our son, is Nathaniel Brodgen; son of Joyce and Eli Brodgen. Put it to rest now, Lupe, put it to rest," she said.

"Yes, my love," he responded.

The next day life on the Outback was back to normal. Lupe and Mama Joyce had Rico controlling the fish market. Rod and Amelia worked on making their house a home.

They were falling back in love again.

Nate worked in the lumberyard. Santiago relocated and decided to go to school closer to home; while Maddie was busy being Maddie. She'd met another bad boy while working at the post office. He too was a biker and a truck driver. He was the all-around bad boy and she loved it! He delivered uniforms to the post office.

One afternoon, he came to pick her up in his big

blue 4x4 pickup. He honked his horn and she came running out of the house. Rico sat under the big oak tree with Lupe and Nate, cleaning fish. Nate noticed the look of disgust on Rico's face. Now that he'd gotten his life together, Maddie no longer seemed interested. However, it was apparent that he loved her.

"Don't worry son, she will come around."

"I'm not so sure about that. One thing for sure, he doesn't deserve her!"

"Just pray, son, just pray for her," suggested Nate.

Maddie and her bad boy went on a two-day getaway, which turned into four. It was on that trip that she was scared straight. He took her places she knew she shouldn't have been in. Each day, he drank himself into a stupor. He promised to take her home, but didn't.

Maddie did the only thing that she knew how to do; she prayed. The sight of her constantly praying killed the vibe of his friends, so they kicked them out.

"I thought you were a social butterfly! A fun girl, kool—not some Jesus freak."

The funny thing was, she wasn't the least offended by his sly remark. All she knew was Jesus. Her parents talked and preached Jesus. At that moment she knew it was him, Jesus, that she needed.

Ironically, Eli happened to bring her home on a Wednesday night, Bible study night.

He whipped his big truck into the yard, with an attitude.

Rico was standing on the porch, just about to

knock on the door. Maddie jumped out of the truck and slammed the door. It took his aggravation to a whole new level.

Eli jumped out and went around to meet her. Grabbing her by her wrist, he began to yell.

"Wait a minute girl, I've just about had enough of you!"

Like lightning, Rico was off the porch and at her side.

"You better take your hands off of her," he warned. "If you're done with her, just leave; but don't put your hands on her!"

"Yeah I'm done, Jesus boy!" he replied, mockingly.

"Yes, I am a Jesus boy and I'll be praying for you!" Rico yelled as the dude jumped back into his truck and sped away.

"I've been praying for you too, ma'am," he added, turning to Maddie.

"Really?"

Maddie looked down to see that he had his Bible in his hand. Man, he had changed! Now it was her turn.

"It looks like you could use a hot shower, some food, and some Jesus Juice."

"Yes, a full cup please," she replied.

"Come on. I know your dad's gonna be relieved to see you."

Just like the Prodigal Son, each time she left Nate always welcomed her home with open arms.

Made in the USA
Columbia, SC
17 May 2022

60514597R00124